MUDDLE AND WIN

The BATTLE of SALLY JONES

Also by John Dickinson

The Cup of the World
The Widow and the King
The Fatal Child
The Lightstep
W.E.

JOHN DICKINSON

David Fickling Books

OXFORD · NEW YORK

31 Beaumont Street
Oxford OX1 2NP, UK

MUDDLE AND WIN
A DAVID FICKLING BOOK 978 0 857 56036 0
Published in Great Britain by David Fickling Books,
A Random House Group Company

This edition published 2012

1 3 5 7 9 10 8 6 4 2

Set in 12/16pt Goudy Old Style

DAVID FICKLING BOOKS
31 Beaumont Street, Oxford, OX1 2NP

www.**kids**at**randomhouse**.co.uk
www.**randomhouse**.co.uk

Addresses for companies within The Random House Group Limited can be
found at: www.randomhouse.co.uk/offices.htm

THE RANDOM HOUSE GROUP Limited Reg. No. 954009

A CIP catalogue record for this book is available from the British Library.

Printed and bound in Great Britain by Clays Ltd, St Ives plc

1: DOWN . . .

Pandemonium is a place. To get there you go down.

That's not 'down' as in the bottom of a mine. You can go to the deepest mine you like and dig and dig and dig until there's so much air pressing on top of you that it squashes you to treacle. But you don't get to Pandemonium that way. It's the *other* sort of down.

Think of your mind like it's a house. What you're looking for is in one of the little rooms at the back. There won't be much light there, and there'll be things scattered all over the floor. Most of it's stuff you've always known about but don't get out and look at too much. You start clearing it to one side. Never mind the dust. Never mind the smell. (Listen – even the best-kept minds have

1

rooms like this.) When you find you're shifting aside thoughts you would never, *ever* try to explain to anybody – and there will be some – then you're in the right place.

Underneath it all, there'll be a trap door. It may have a padlock on it. It may be marked with mystic runes or with bright black-and-yellow stickers that say DANGER! DON'T GO HERE! Or it may already be open. It depends what sort of mind you have.

If it's locked, you open it. You have the key, of course.

The trap door opens onto darkness. There are no steps. No lift, no ladder, not even a rope. You just step over the void and drop.

And you fall. Your stomach goes hollow and hits the back of your throat. The darkness rushes up past you like wind, faster and faster. There's a tingling in your feet because they're standing on nothing. Above you, the trap door has already dwindled to a point of light as small as a distant star. You think you're going to hit the bottom at any moment and be squashed. But there *is* no bottom.

Still you fall, faster and faster! You're sorry you did this now, but there's no going back. You can't see anything. There's nothing to feel or hear except the rush of the darkness. Maybe you aren't even falling any more, but just hanging there with all that nothingness blasting up past you.

It goes on like that. On and on. And it's beginning to get warm.

For most people, going to Pandemonium is a one-way trip. You probably didn't want to know that. But of course *you'll* come back. (You hope.)

Now look down! You see it – a dull glow spreading below your feet. Not flames, but a kind of slow, black-red pulse like the embers of a huge fire. You're getting somewhere at last.

You don't look at the glow itself, already swelling as you rush towards it. That comes from a *long* way down. You're not going that far this time. You keep your eyes fixed around the edges, where the shapes of huge towers have begun to appear, rising like rockets towards you as you fall. They're built of brass and domed with metals that gleam dully in the furnace light. There are cupolas and turrets and battlements and hanging gardens where nothing grows but branches of hammered gold. There are bell towers and terraces and ziggurats and monuments and arches and staircases as wide as football pitches that do nothing but go down, down, down.

Speaking of which . . . *Start running!*

You're careering down a huge staircase – so steep that really you're still falling as you run, your legs clattering madly as they try to keep up with the rest of you! Shapes whirl past in the gloom – buildings, pillars, the glow of a furnace, glimpsed and gone in a moment. More and more of them. It's like a huge city built on a slope that falls for ever downwards, and you're a train coming into the station. Your feet are bruised, your lungs are gasping, but your speed's easing. Not quite so mad now. You can almost control it. In fact, you'd *better* control it because the stairs are ending. There's level ground ahead, ground that you hit stumbling, pitching to the floor (ouch!) where you lie gasping and feeling sick for long moments before you can finally lift your head.

Now.

Pick yourself up, and look at Pandemonium.

You're in an alley, of sorts, between two huge buildings. On either side are rows of great arches with nothing but blackness behind them. They yawn wide, as if they are mouths about to swallow you. It feels like being caught in the middle of a pack of giant stone tigers. Or flesh-eating ghouls, perhaps.

The air is warm enough to make you sweat. It smells of hot metal and it's humming with sounds. You can't quite hear what they are, but you can feel them crawling on your skin. Sounds like gongs, maybe drums, crowds murmuring. And yes, faint screams.

Don't worry. You'll be quite safe. Somewhere, you've got some rules for staying alive in Pandemonium. Let's have a look . . .

RULES FOR STAYING ALIVE IN PANDEMONIUM

1. DON'T EVER GO THERE. DON'T EVER *THINK* OF GOING THERE. LOOK, YOU REALLY, REALLY DON'T WANT TO KNOW. THE PEOPLE AREN'T FRIENDLY. AT ALL. IN FACT, IT'S STRETCHING A POINT TO CALL THEM 'PEOPLE' . . .

(Whoops! Blown that one. What else does it say?)

. . . ENTRAILS WITH RED-HOT FORKS AND SPLIT YOUR TONGUE WITH RAZORS AND PULL OUT EVERY ONE OF YOUR FINGERNAILS *VERY SLOWLY*

5

AND THEN THEY'LL FLAY YOUR SKIN OFF WITH ESPECIALLY BLUNT KNIVES WHILE LISTENING TO CHEESY POP MUSIC – AND THAT'S JUST THE FIRST MORNING, OK?

2. ALL RIGHT, SO YOU'VE BROKEN RULE 1. SACK YOUR TRAVEL AGENT. MEANWHILE, IF YOU WANT TO LIVE TO SEE YOUR TRAVEL AGENT AGAIN, *LOOK AS THOUGH YOU'RE MEANT TO BE THERE.* ALWAYS TRY TO LOOK AS THOUGH YOU'RE IN A HURRY AND YOU'VE BEEN SENT BY SOMEONE IMPORTANT.

3. IF YOU MEET ANYONE, DON'T SPEAK TO THEM. DON'T LOOK THEM IN THE EYES. (IF THEY HAVE EYES. SOME OF THEM HAVEN'T.)

4. DON'T ASSUME YOU CAN'T BE SEEN, EVEN WHEN YOU'RE IN SHADOW. YOU CAN BE. SEE THAT ARCHED WINDOW UP THERE, LIKE A MOUTH IN THAT TOWER?

Er . . .

Window?

There *is* a window up there. Creepy.

. . . THERE'S SOMEONE IN THERE. YOU CAN'T SEE THEM, BUT THEY'RE THERE, ALL RIGHT. THEY'RE WATCHING YOU. THEY'RE BEGINNING TO WONDER. YOU NEED TO MOVE. *NOW.*

Move. Quickly. Think: *I'm meant to be here. I've been sent by someone important. And bad-tempered. Nobody mess with me, OK?* Keep thinking that. Your footsteps make an ugly, metallic sound on the paving. That's because the paving isn't stone. It's brass. They like brass here.

At the end of the alley there's a smaller building that looks a bit like a chapel. There's a round-arched doorway covered with carvings which . . .

. . . On a hurried look, seems to be illustrating exactly what happens to anyone caught breaking Rule 1 down here.

And on a closer look . . .

Yup. Whatever this little building is, it's definitely *not* a chapel. And whoever built it has a twisted sense of humour.

Round the corner. A big terrace. It seems empty, but take no chances. Don't run – just move quickly. Beyond the balcony you can see the towers and battlements and domes of the next level of palaces. They're even bigger than the ones around you. Pandemonium's built on a slope. The further down the slope a person lives, the more important they are. That's how it works here.

The palace in front of you has twisty turrets and curvy, pointy roofs like horns. It's six storeys high and walled in brass. The windows are great open arches framed with zigzag tooth carvings. They glow with the light of a huge fire within. The person who lives there likes fire. His sort often do.

You look through the window. He's got a visitor. The visitor doesn't want to be there. Right now, he wants to be anywhere else but where he is. His huge eyes are popping, bouncing a little like ping-pong balls in his leathery skull. There's sweat on his green-grey skin, running down his domed forehead and dripping from his pointy nose. His big, bat-like ears flap in distress. His mouth is gaping, pleading. He's begging for mercy, but down here using the word 'mercy' is like trying to put out a Bunsen burner with a tube of ethanol. (Sometimes literally. They really do like fire here.)

He struggles, but he can't escape. He's held by two great, grinning fiends, each bigger by half than he is. His desperate eyes roll upwards to the ceiling. He sees, with sudden clearness, the intricate, writhing, oh-so-funny carvings there, richly painted in colours and gold leaf to bring out just how funny they are. And with his last thought he thinks – as a brass hammer the size of a cathedral bell-clapper blocks it all from view – that they're *not funny at all*.

Don't look!

SPLAT!

Ugh.

Poor devil.

There's no visitor now, in the palace of the curvy teeth. There's a bit more decoration on the ceiling, though. There's some on the walls and floor too. And scattered around the room . . .

Well, that's about half of his chin, over there by the fireplace.

There's one of his eyes, rolling gently across the floor.

That's one of his arms.

So is that.

So is that.

You've no idea what *that* bit is . . .

And the air is filled with the laughter of the two fiends, who a moment before had been holding the smaller fiend between them. It's loud laughter, because they find this sort of thing very funny indeed. And it has that added little note to it which makes you think, maybe, that they're laughing extra loud and extra long on purpose, to please the person who wields the hammer, and to make it just a little less likely that one day they might be under the hammer themselves.

They troop out, still cackling, to the tap-rattle-tap accompaniment of their knuckles trailing along the floor. Their laughter echoes down long hallways of glowing brass, fading, seeming now to come from all around. Blending with the pervasive hum that isn't so much heard as felt upon the skin.

It's another day in Pandemonium.

2: MUDDLESPOT

The wielder of the hammer was not laughing.

'Tiresome,' he said aloud.

He had a voice like layers and layers of dark, cunningly folded velvet, with all sorts of pockets and corners in which little meanings might be hidden. It was the kind of voice that could make something very little seem rather a lot. And when he sighed, as he did now, the light in the room flickered.

He gathered his rich red robes about him and went to pose before a brass mirror. He wanted to look at something soothing. He was, of course, quite beautiful. His hair was black, gleaming and flowing, curling to fall over the high collar of his cloak. His skin was smooth, his nose straight but not too long. His brows were strong and so was his jaw, on which

11

he allowed a fine stubble to grow, as if he didn't really care how he looked but just happened to be beautiful anyway.

His eyes were a little larger than they should have been, and they were very, very deep. They were the sort of eyes that you might not so much *look* into as *fall* into. And once there you would just go round and round, in the alternating light and darkness, until you forgot even your own name. And when you had forgotten that, you would never come out.

He did not have horns, unlike some of his kind. He did not wear a crown or a coronet either. He did not need to. He simply chose to look beautiful. And he chose that his fiends should all look appallingly ugly, to remind himself, and anyone who saw him, just how beautiful he was.

He also chose that he should be at least four times the size of anyone who worked for him. Size gets you respect, in Pandemonium. And the bright bronze hammer the size of a cathedral bell-clapper, which had just disappeared back inside his robes – yes, that helped too.

(His name? You'll need to know it. Here . . .

Corozin

Don't use it more than you have to, and don't say it aloud, more than you can help. It's *really* better not to.)

He looked at himself in the mirror for a while. Then he lifted his hand, curling his long, beautiful fingers just a little to show that he was sensitive as well as strong. And he looked at himself again.

Ah, yes. It was a heart-meltingly beautiful sight. Or would have been, if he had had a heart.

He shifted his feet. Something went *squelch!* The brass floor of his chamber was still littered with bits of his unfortunate visitor. One bloodshot, bulbous eyeball peered up at him, wobbling slightly. He sighed again.

'Muddlespot.'

A tiny imp appeared, somewhere down at floor level. He was carrying a brush that was almost as tall as he was, and a dustpan that was half again as wide. Both brush and pan were made of brass, of course. Even the bristles of the brush were brass.

'Clear this up.'

And Corozin went back to admiring himself in the mirror.

The imp was a *very* little imp. His head and body were like two wrinkled peas, of which the slightly smaller one was balanced on top of the larger. He had a long nose and big ears, but his arms were silly little things like the forelimbs of a miniature T. rex and his legs were barely long enough to lift his dumpy body off the floor. Tufts of ginger hair, thick as spines, grew here and there on his grey skin. His eyes were bright and beady. On his head he wore a round red pillbox hat.

He looked around the room. He pursed his little lips and eyed the body parts scattered across the floor. It was an eight, he decided. An eight out of ten. The boss must have been upset. Teeth didn't normally get embedded in the brass wall.

The imp was used to clearing up after these little events. In fact, he himself had been born in one. It had been soon after Corozin's former boss had been hauled off down to the lower circles and Corozin had become the boss instead. Someone had disappointed him, had come here and gone *splat* under the hammer, and ended up in bits all over the floor. And Corozin had looked at the mess in distaste.

Then he had picked up one grey, leathery and now-quite-squishy body part in his beautiful long hands. He had selected one hairy, juicy wart, pinched it off the skin and spat upon it. Immediately, the wart had swelled up by a factor of about ten, grown a head, four limbs, ears, nose and a pair of bright beady eyes. It had even grown the little pillbox hat.

It had become an imp. A very little little devil. And Corozin had said to it, 'You are Muddlespot.'

'Yes, Your Serenity,' Muddlespot had answered brightly.

'Clear this up.'

And clearing up was what Muddlespot did. He did not mind the mess. He had got used to the ickiness of it. First he took the big bits and dropped them out of the window. Then he got the brush and swept the loose little bits into his pan, and they went out of the window too. After that he mopped up the squidgy stuff, and burnished the brass floor with the brass bristles of his brush until it shone and no stain was to be seen. Finally he prised out the bits that had got stuck here and there, and beat the brass back into shape with his own little hammer, until it was all smooth and he could polish over those places too.

He did it carefully and well. It was his job. He *liked* being good at the job. He liked the *zing* of his brass-bristled brush across the brass surfaces, and the way dented, stained metal would glow back into life again with a little rubbing and attention. It made him feel useful. It made him feel he was wanted, and would go on being wanted for as long as Corozin went on being disappointed in people.

And there was no sign of that changing. In fact, it had been happening rather more than usual just lately. That pile of bits under the window was getting quite large. Soon he'd have to climb up to the next floor, just to be able to carry on dropping things on top of it.

Whisper it low, but Muddlespot was *happy*. What's more, he was getting away with it, which doesn't often happen in Pandemonium. But that's because he was small and no one paid him much attention.

Unless they had a reason.

'Muddlespot?'

'Er . . . yes, Your Serenity?'

Corozin frowned. It was, he admitted to himself, a desperate measure. It had about as much chance as trying to run a ski slope on the lower reaches of Pande-monium. Snowballs in hell. Warts and success. Some things just *didn't* go together.

But for the time being at least, it wasn't about success. It was about not admitting failure. It was about Being Seen To Be Doing Something. And if he didn't do something pretty quickly, he was going to find himself under a hammer that would make his own look like a hand-me-down from Tinkerbell.

He reached down with his finger and thumb, picked up the little imp by the scruff of his neck and held him at eye level. 'You're not busy, are you?'

The position Muddlespot now occupied was like someone who had been caught on the hook of a giant construction crane and hoisted up about twenty storeys with the crane driver grinning madly at him from inside the cab. The soles of his feet tingled at the thought of the drop below. He had a strong feeling that what he said next would be very, very important. And that 'Yes' was definitely the wrong answer. And that 'No' was almost certainly wrong too. His hands still clutched his dustpan and brush. In the pan lay two-thirds of the dead fiend's nostril (and also some of its contents). The nostril rocked, gently.

'I'm clearing up the mess, Your Serenity,' he squeaked.

(That's another of those little rules for Staying Alive in Pandemonium:

. . . ALWAYS TELL THEM WHAT THEY ALREADY KNOW. KEEP TELLING IT. DON'T CHANGE

YOUR STORY. WHATEVER YOU DO, *DON'T* SAY ANYTHING THAT THEY MIGHT THINK IS INTERESTING . . .

Muddlespot hadn't been out of the palace much, but he'd learned from watching the mistakes of those who strayed into it. Mistake Number One being to attract the boss's attention in the first place. Quite often, that was all it took.)

'Muddlespot,' purred Corozin in his most soothing tones. 'How many times? It's Ssse-*rehni*ty. Like that. Slur it, E to E flat, just gracefully. You can do that, can't you?'

'Yes, Your Sere-e-enity!' piped Muddlespot, who was born from a wart and had the musical ability to match.

Corozin winced. 'I think you said you *weren't* busy, didn't you?'

'I'm just clearing up the—'

'Oh, *sssup*er! I'm so glad you're available. I have a job for you. Congratulations, Muddlespot. I'm going to give you your chance. Your big break.'

'You're . . . sending me up?' said Muddlespot, like a comfortable headquarters clerk who has just been told of his transfer to a badly mauled rifle battalion camped out in the shell-holes where he is assured of honour, glory, death and frostbite.

'Pressisely. On a mission of highest importance.'

Muddlespot wilted. The nostril of his former colleague rolled off his pan and disappeared silently into the void beneath his feet.

'I'm convinced you have the right qualities,' said Corozin, releasing him. 'Guards!'

Muddlespot fell all the way to the brass floor, where, still being essentially wart-like, he bounced two or three times. When he had stopped doing that and had picked himself up, he found that the two knuckle-dragging fiends had re-entered the room.

'Our new agent,' came Corozin's voice from on high. 'For Mission Alpha.'

The guards peered down at him. They were smaller than their master, but still a *lot* bigger than Muddlespot. They had fangs about as long as Muddlespot was tall. They had talons like iron stakes. Their eyes glowed hotly in their grey-black skin.

'*Muddlespot?!?*' cried one of them.

'Oh, that's a good one!' guffawed the other. 'That's a *good* one, Your Serenity, that is!'

'You mistake me,' said Corozin, with just that slight drop in his voice that signalled instant danger. The guards stopped laughing at once. They stood to attention.

'I've been watching our young friend for some time,' Corozin said. He turned to the window, searching his mind for anything good that could be said about someone who was both a wart and a gobbet-raker. 'He's very, er, diligent. Obedient. That's what we need . . .

'Besides,' he added, leaning out over the balcony and observing that the pile of heads, limbs, torsos and entrails of his former agents had grown remarkably since he had last looked at it. 'Besides, for some reason we seem to be rather short of operatives at the moment. Unless one of you two would like to volunteer?'

'Oh *no*, Your Serenity!'

'We wouldn't dream . . .'

'Pressisely,' said Corozin. 'Take him away and prepare him.'

'Er, Your Serenity?' squeaked Muddlespot, as a guard scooped him up in one claw.

'*Thank* you, Muddlespot. I look forward to your report of success on Mission Alpha . . .'

'But Your Serenity . . .'

Corozin flashed his most charming smile. '. . . I *really* wouldn't bother to report anything else.'

'Come on, Muddlespot,' growled the guard.

They left their lord admiring himself in the mirror of brass. They ambled down long, sonorous brass corridors and under arches of brass that were decorated with shiny pointed teeth of brass. Muddlespot went with them. He didn't have much choice. He was about the size of a squash-ball in their claws.

Very like a squash-ball. They even bounced him a couple of times off the floor without thinking about it. He left nasty smudgy marks on the shiny brass carpet, which he would have to clean up later if he ever got a 'later' in which to do it.

3: MISSION ALPHA

Muddlespot peered out fearfully between the talons of the guards. His eyes had stopped rattling in his skull, but his knees were still knocking and his skin was covered in goose bumps. They were in a long, long torchlit corridor that was floored and walled with brass, and every inch of brass writhed with carvings. The carvings were exactly the same sort of thing that decorated the walls and ceilings of Corozin's chamber – detailed, explicit and oh-so-*very*-humorous, if you found that kind of thing funny, which just at that moment Muddlespot didn't at all. He wished the guards would stop sniggering. They made a noise like forks scraping on plates. The sound of it was giving him toothache.

'Here we are, Muddlespot!' they cried, ducking

through a low doorway framed with yet more carved teeth. 'Briefing room!'

The briefing room was small and badly lit. There was very little free floor space, and most of it was taken up with a grille through which rose ill-smelling fumes and the sound of ominous glopping. The guards were very careful to walk around this when they entered.

In one corner stood a standard No. 3 'Gobbelin' Utility Furnace (an ageing but very reliable model). Stacked against it was a full set of pokers of various sizes, some of which were dull from under-use and some – plainly the guards' favourites – were also dull, but in a rather suspicious way that suggested they might have been really smooth and shiny if it hadn't been that the things they got used for tended to put a bit of a stain on them.

On the other side of the furnace was a range of pincers, also arranged in order of size but missing the No. 7 from the set, because of that time when one of the guards had got it a little bit *too* white-hot and had then used a little *too* much force to extract whatever it was he had been extracting from the unfortunate person he had been entertaining at the time.

There were three mangles of different grades,

two of which were broken and pushed against a wall awaiting repair.

There was the usual array of boots (the ones with spikes on the inside), thumbscrews, saws, nose hooks and entrail forks all piled up together. Many of these were stained, too.

There were stains on the floor, on the walls, on the ceiling. Of course the guards could have got Muddle-spot to come and wipe the stains away any time they wanted. But they didn't. The stains added to the experience, they said. There was nothing like having a few stains to look at while you were being strapped down, they said. Just to let your imagination work a little before things *really* got started.

It was a bit like having a cup of tea, they said. It helps the flavour if you don't wash the pot.

(That's what they *said*. Really, it wasn't like having a cup of tea at all.)

Muddlespot wore the fixed expression of somebody who knows there's only one way out. And it's down the booby-trapped passage, across the snake pit, over the boiling oil and past the poisonous spider whose boot size was way bigger than his own. Whatever he did now, he just wasn't going to make it.

'Agent Muddlespot,' intoned one of the guards.

'The information you are about to receive is for your ears only. It must never be revealed to anyone but the three of us and the boss himself. And we already know it, so don't bother.'

'And it's better not to talk to the boss about it unless he asks you,' muttered the other guard. 'Just in case he gets funny about it.'

(You will notice that neither of them used Corozin's name. And by *funny*, of course, they meant . . . Ah, but you've understood that now, haven't you?)

They opened the furnace and plonked Muddle-spot down in front of it. One of them busily worked the bellows until the dull red coals brightened to a white glare. The other produced a tub of evil-smelling powder, tipped a small amount of it into one hand, murmured some words and then spat upon it. He dipped a claw in it and drew signs in the air before the furnace. Lines of fire trailed from his finger like the light from a sparkler, turning from white-gold to green and then a dull purple. When he had finished, he murmured some more words and threw the remaining powder into the furnace. The flames huffed briefly and died again.

'Give it a kick,' said the guard on the bellows.

The other guard grunted, picked up a particularly heavy-looking poker and went *Whangngngg-gng-g!!!* with it on the side of the furnace.

Nothing happened, except that the poker bent.

'Give it a—' the first guard began again. But he was interrupted by a *huff!* from the flames. They grew brighter in some spots and darker in others. Muddle-spot peered closely.

It was almost as if pictures were forming in the furnace, but they were too fuzzy for him to see what they showed. Also, he had a feeling that they weren't just pictures he was seeing. Some of them might have been eyes, looking back at him.

'It needs tuning,' said the first guard. 'Give it—'

Before he could finish, the pictures sharpened. Muddlespot saw that they were buildings – not the sort of buildings he knew in Pandemonium, but smaller ones; squat, plain and built (crazy!) with very little metal of any kind and *no brass at all*. He was looking at a row of houses in the place Up There. The place that some people called 'Earth'.

'That's better,' said one of his briefers. 'Agent Muddlespot, have you ever seen this before?'

'No, sir.'

'Then take a good look. Because this is *it*. This is

Darlington Row. Corozin's patch. Note the school and the corner shop . . .'

'Key points,' said his colleague.

'. . . And the houses down to the Green, where our turf ends and Trapezius's lot take over.'

(Trapezius was the owner of the next palace along on this level of Pandemonium. Between his staff and Corozin's there existed the usual friendly rivalry that found its expression in back-stabbing, disembowelling and dunking each other in buckets of acid whenever there wasn't anything better to do.)

The scene reeled slowly past, as if the three of them were seeing out through the eyes of somebody who was standing on the street corner and looking obligingly up and down the road.

'It's average human stuff. Some good, some bad. Some downright virtuous. There's no special potential. We have to graft hard for what we get.'

'We win some, we lose some,' said the other guard. 'You know how it goes.'

'Until lately, we've been able to make up our quota and Low Command hasn't complained too much. But now there's a problem.'

'A big one.'

Muddlespot's skin tingled. Suddenly he understood

why Corozin had been disappointed with so many of his agents of late. Something had been going wrong up on Earth. Somebody up there had been handing out defeat after defeat after defeat to all Corozin's best and finest devils. They had gone up one after another, and one after another they had failed. The object of Mission Alpha was . . .

The picture changed.

'It's *Sally Jones*,' said the guard.

4: SALLY

The bell had gone. The school yard and the pavements outside the gates were teeming with young escapees. Sally was among them with her bag over one shoulder. It was a heavy bag, with a mountain of homework in it. She passed Ameena and Janey and Chris, who were swapping tunes on their mobiles.

'Hi, Sally!' they said to her.

'Hi, guys!'

'Seeya tomorrow.'

'Yeah, seeya.'

Ameena and Janey and Chris were each nearly six feet tall, and won tennis matches at county level and competed in the district high jump. Janey was also a showjumper and was seriously good at that too. Sally wasn't one of the sporty set at Darlington

High. But they all said 'Hi' to her because she was Sally.

At the school gates Mrs Watkins, Head of Languages, gave her a wan smile. Mrs Watkins was still heartbroken because Sally had decided to drop Spanish at the start of Year 9. What she didn't yet know was that Sally was planning to join the Japanese club she ran at lunch times as a way of making it up to her. (OK, it'd mean another language to learn, but so what? Japanese wasn't going to be a problem for Sally.)

On the pavement, Cassie Anderson-Higgs had draped herself languidly against a parking meter. 'So I mean, like, pleeeeease!' she yawned. 'Not only was it a hamburger, but he'd got them to put mayo on it! So I told him – "Right, you're dumped, jerkface. And by the way, you kiss like a fish." Oh – hi, Sally!'

'Oh – *hi*, Sally!' called Viola and Carmela and Imogen Grey, looking round.

Cassie and her group were the '14/18' set at Darlington High. They weren't just wannabe eighteen-year-olds. They *were* eighteen in every sense except the technical one involving the calendar. Including how they looked, where they went and what they drank when they got there. Cassie dumped six men a week. Viola was taking driving lessons. Their contempt for anyone else was Total. The attention they gave them was Nil. Except for Sally. They liked Sally.

It was easy to like Sally. She had an open, uncomplicated face and she smiled a lot. Her forehead was large, her eyebrows were strong and her nose and chin were small, so that it looked as if she carried her head tilted slightly forward all the time. Her hair was dark, trimmed in a neat line over her eyes and to collar length at the back. She wasn't a fashion leader, or follower. She wasn't a sports hero. She wasn't the centre of any of the social sets in her year, and she wasn't ever going to be lead singer in the school band. What's more, she was getting awesome grades in class without ever seeming to try. But nobody minded.

Because if your phone was out of credit, you could borrow Sally's. If you'd left your maths homework at school, you could call Sally and she would give you the questions. If you called her after 7 p.m., she could probably give you the answers too. Her allowance wasn't great, but if you needed any of it, it was yours. She'd hear your lines for the school play. And when all was lost and the Head of Year was bearing down on you and your last alibi was blown, Sally would get you out of it. Somehow. Without even lying.

If you needed to cry about anything, you could

cry on Sally's shoulder. She'd listen. Later you might realize that in fact she'd been in a screaming rush about something else, but she'd stopped for you and had got the something else done afterwards. She'd stop for anybody. Even for ex-Cassiemen who thought she might be able to get them back in with Cassie. (Some hope.)

And she never lost it.

Ever.

Though it's true that lately things had been changing a little, without Sally or anyone really noticing.

For example, her relationship with her alarm clock wasn't so good any more. Back in her first year at the school it had been her best friend. But over time, morning after morning, it had become more of an 'Oh – you again?' Soon it would descend through those same stages of Pain → Toothgrindingly Irritating → Formally Dumped that every Cassieman came to know. (Except that with Sally the process would take months. A Cassieman could get the lot in five minutes: Love → → Pain → → TI → → FD!)

And then there was . . .

'Oi! Sally! YOUR BOYFRIEND'S WAVING AT YOU!'

. . . There was Billie, her non-identical twin sister, who right at this moment was walking no more than six feet behind her and *still* felt she had to sound off like a passenger ferry in fog. Sally looked round. (So did half the street.) But it turned out that the 'boyfriend' wasn't Stevie, and it wasn't Mac either. Too bad. Stevie and Mac were both ex-Cassiemen that Sally thought were actually quite nice.

It was Charlie B, waving from the bus stop forty metres down Garrick Way. And now Sally had to choose between 1) not waving back at Charlie, and 2) letting every one of the four hundred schoolchildren, teachers, parents, motorists, pedestrians and pensioners within earshot of Billie think that Charlie B was indeed her boyfriend.

She chose 2) and waved back.

Charlie grinned, waved enthusiastically and then turned to his mates, who pounced on him at once about his suddenly discovered love life. Sally shrugged. They'd do their worst, but hey. Boys were no good at rumour.

'I don't see why you don't dump him,' complained Billie, trailing behind her down Darlington Row.

'He's not mine to dump,' said Sally.

'He's *fat*! He *gorges* on chips. He eats the batter off the cod and leaves the fish! Cod are nearly *extinct*!'

'They're not extinct. They're overfished. Hi, Mr Granger.'

Mr Granger was one of Darlington Row's army of pensioners. He was doddering along the pavement in the wake of his ancient terrier, which he had probably found mummified in the tomb of an Egyptian pharaoh at the turn of some century or other, and which hadn't got any younger since. Mr Granger wore baggy leather shorts and knee-length socks and a hat that he touched when he spoke.

'Hello, hello!' he said, touching his hat. 'Going home from school?'

'No, we've just landed from Mars,' said Billie, deadpan.

'That's right, Mr Granger,' said Sally, meaning school, not Mars.

'Jolly good!'

'Darling Charlie!' fluted Billie in a high voice, pursuing Sally on down the pavement. 'That's you. "Darling Charlie!" He's a balloon! A great big squelching turnip! He doesn't walk so much as waddle! I hope you wipe your lips after you kiss him because they'll be all smeary with grease!'

'I showed him how to multiply fractions. He didn't get it. Now he does.'

'Oh, *fractions*! Is that what you call it? You should *show* him how to do a bleep test or two!'

'He can't help his shape,' said Sally, waving again as the number 86 bus roared past them with Charlie B at the window.

'He could try,' muttered Billie.

Sally knew Charlie could try harder than he did. But she also knew he wasn't going to. He got quite a lot from the other kids about it and he still wasn't going to, so it wouldn't make anything better if she got at him as well.

Besides, bleep tests, which she had once enjoyed, were now on much the same curve as her alarm clock. That was another thing that was changing for Sally.

The number 86 receded down Darlington Row, bearing with it the face that lunched a thousand chips.

A *schoolgirl*?

Muddlespot fell off his perch.

He bounced on the floor a couple of times and

sat there with his eyes wobbling and little circles of twittering green ghouls floating around his head.

He had been expecting someone of immense power and holiness. A terrible enemy, who had defeated all of Corozin's best. A threat to the very fabric of Pandemonium. A saint. A martyr. Maybe even a lama.

Maybe the schoolgirl *was* a lama?

To tell the truth, he was not sure exactly what a lama was and whether you would find one in Darlington Row. The rumours that filtered down as far as Corozin's palace made him shudder, but were never terribly specific. He had had what you might call a sheltered existence – up to now.

'Pay attention, Agent Muddlespot!' said one of the guards, plonking him back on the rim of the furnace.

The other guard had picked up a standard No. 3 red-hot poker and was using it as a pointing stick. 'Notice the shoes – no scuffs. The tie knotted at the top button, see? And the things you don't see. She's vegetarian. Helps injured animals. Visits the old man down the street who can't get out any more. Alarm bells ringing yet?'

'Er . . .'

'Better brush up on that fieldwork, Agent.'

'Ve-ry quickly,' agreed the other.

(Neither of them, of course, had done any field-work of their own since the days of buckled shoes and powdered wigs. And they weren't going to do any more if they could help it. Doing what they did down here was easier and safer. And far more Fun.)

'Just check out her stats,' said one grimly.

Another pinch of powder went into the furnace. *Huff!* Little figures of fire were leaping and dancing across the image of the girl in the flames. Muddle-spot knew what they were. They were the schoolgirl's Lifetime Deed Counter (LDC).

Everyone Up There had an LDC. And for all of them, a time came when their totals of good and bad deeds could be compared. There then followed a complicated series of adjustments, weightings, appeals, swaps, derivatives, salvations and redemptions which nobody really understood *but* the basic idea was that if the good deed count was low enough and the bad deed count was high enough then the person in question came Down Here and a Lot of Fun was had in chambers like this one, for a Very Long Time.

This LDC said:

Lifetime Good Deeds: 3,971,567
Lifetime Bad Deeds: NIL

Muddlespot whistled. It didn't look as though there was going to be much Fun with Sally Jones. With figures like that, the only source of Fun would be whoever it was who hadn't been able to make them better.

'Er – is there a fault in the counter?'

'Never ask that question, kid,' said one guard.

'Low Command gets stressed when you ask about the LDCs . . .'

'We sent old Filharmouzh down there to tell them there *had* to be a fault. He came back in pieces. I mean, *very small* pieces. When we undid the packet . . .' The guard pulled a face. 'Well, we couldn't help it.'

'We breathed him in. Bits of him, anyway.'

'He was mostly dust, see.'

'Made me sneeze, he did.'

'Thing is, the LDCs aren't run by Low Command. It's more of a Joint Commission kind of thing. With the Other Side. They're a teeny bit sensitive about that down below. So no, you don't ask. The LDC tells it like it is. Nil means Nil. Believe it.'

Billie dashed to get through the front garden gate ahead of Sally. '*I'm* on the computer!' she said.

The computer had been imported into the house

by Greg, Mum's partner. It stood on the upstairs landing, which was the only space that Mum would allow it. Once Greg got home he would monopolize it for the rest of the evening. The two-hour window between the girls' return from school and Greg's from work was very precious.

'Fine,' sighed Sally, and waited while Billie hunted for her house key. She reckoned up the chances of getting five uninterrupted minutes on Wikipedia that evening, and decided there might not be any. Her bag felt that bit heavier, as if the mountain of homework had just added another crag to itself.

Twenty seconds later, she was still waiting. Billie lost her key at least once a month. It looked like she'd lost it today, too.

Sally reached for her own key.

'Found it!' cried Billie. She opened the door and dashed up the stairs to the landing. Sally followed her into the hall.

There was a smell of smoke in the house, so Mum must be home early and trying to cook. Mum coming home early usually meant . . .

'Hi there,' said Mum, poking her head round the kitchen door. And yes, she was looking harassed all right. Mum was slim and blonde, and, given a peaceful hour to wash, dress and apply make-up, could look very elegant. But she managed an office at work and a family at home, and between the two of them they didn't leave many peaceful hours in her week. Most of the time, she lived with bags under her eyes and a faint air of panic. *'I'm sorry darling, I can't right now'* was one of the things she said a lot. She had a string of other things that she also said a lot, but they got you into trouble if you used any of them yourself.

'Hi, Mum. Tough day?'

'You've *no* idea,' said Mum. 'Stood it till three and then couldn't take it any more. King-sized headache. A million and one things to do, and of course I've promised I'd do cakes for the PTA raffle and the wretched *oven's* playing up again . . .'

'Like a hand with that?' said Sally.

She said it even though her bag-carrying shoulder complained that her evening was already looking full. She said it at once, because Baking With Mum had always been a special thing, and it didn't happen so much these days because Mum was always run off her feet.

'That'd be great, sweetheart,' said Mum, also at once. 'In fact, could you do it for me?'

'Oh,' said Sally.

'You'll have to watch them like a hawk. The thermostat's playing up again. I've ruined one lot already.'

'Sure,' said Sally.

So the evening's to-do list now began: 1) Bake cakes for the PTA, assisted by dodgy oven. Followed by, 2) Do mountain of homework, unassisted by Wikipedia. Plus she couldn't get started on homework at the same time as baking because the oven was dodgy enough for her to have to keep an eye on it throughout. She knew all about the thermostat and its little ways.

It was like a lot of things at home – things that almost didn't quite work and had to be jiggled or coaxed or teased very, very carefully until they did. Mum just didn't have time to get them all mended. Or organized. Or clean.

1) Bake cakes. OK. Bring it on. (Though it would have been nice to do something with Mum for a change.)

'Thanks,' said Mum. 'Thanks so much, sweetheart. I *keep* telling Greg he's got to get it fixed . . .' She paused. Her eyes went a little unfocused, as they do when a busy person is trying to remember what they were going to do next. The air of stress and frazzle lifted, just a little.

Then it came on again, full force. '*Billie!* How many times have I told you? WIPE YOUR FEET WHEN YOU COME IN!'

From above, Billie wailed. 'Oh, *what?*'

Sally checked her shoes. She thought she remembered wiping them on the mat, but she couldn't be sure. There was a small amount of dirt caught in the angle of one heel. So to be on the safe side . . .

'That might have been me, Mum. I'll clean it up.'

The jingle of the newly-woken computer sniggered from upstairs.

'Did you *see* that?' cried one of the guards. 'She *covered* for her *sister!* I mean – what can you do? What can you *do?!*'

'Sends shivers up your spine,' agreed the other, licking his lips. 'Eh, Muddlespot?'

Muddlespot was the stuff of Pandemonium. He was Pandemonium to his very last pimple. He knew that the whole point of everything was to get to the people Up There and work the LDCs until you could get them back Down Here and have all sorts of Fun with them. That was the way it was. He thought about it as much as someone in a fishing village thinks about fishing. That is, rather a lot, and in just one way.

But even in Pandemonium, what you do *is* somehow what you are. Muddlespot did cleaning. He was a cleaner. He didn't really get to share in the Fun, any more than he got to share in the Disappointments. He just got to clean up after both. His world existed in the bit between the screams and the gleams. So far as he was concerned, the only *real* difference between Fun and Disappointment was who it was you scraped up afterwards.

And no one down here would *ever* say that this or that stain was their fault, not his. And they would *never* offer to clean it up for him.

That. Just. Wouldn't. Happen.

It had never occurred to him that it ever possibly could.

Those words, *'That might have been me, Mum . . .'* were still spiralling around inside his head like a scent from a garden he had never known existed. He felt a bit dazed.

'Er, yes,' he mumbled. And then he added, 'Scary!'

It was definitely scary. The LDC now read:

Lifetime Good Deeds: 3,971,570
Lifetime Bad Deeds: NILnilNILnilNILnilNILnil

'She's affecting the whole sector,' sniffed a guard. 'Look . . .'

The scene changed. In a room, somewhere else in Darlington Row, Sally was playing a violin. She played it smoothly, easily. The notes had a richness, like polish laid down in many layers of practice. She might never be a maestro, but she was on her way to a sure-fire Distinction at Grade Five, and maybe more than that if she could find the time.

Across the room a small, middle-aged woman was listening. There was a peaceful, almost dreamy look in her eyes. Her thoughts were plain for Muddlespot to see. She had troubles but they were suddenly looking smaller. The fights with people in offices about money, with parents who wanted stardom for their children, with children who could take or leave stardom but didn't see that it had anything to do with playing the A-major scale ten times a week . . . The awful, weary greyness of getting up each morning to another day of it was forgotten. Strength was coming back again. It could be handled. Something good could be made of it all.

Sally, whispered the flames. *Sally makes it worth-while.*

And the LDC read:

Lifetime Bad Deeds: NILcomeonguyswhereareyou?

'She's Big Trouble, Muddlespot. The Enemy have got her. And they've got plans.'

'She's closely guarded, under Sleepless Watch. I tell you, Low Command is worried. They want something done.'

'And if it isn't . . .'

There was a short silence in the briefing room. It was the sort of silence that felt horribly like the descent of a huge brass hammer.

'Your mission, Agent Muddlespot. Infiltrate. Contact. Arrange defection. We'll handle everything else.'

Muddlespot squinted at the flames. He wondered how many agents had been sent on Mission Alpha before him. And what had happened to them. And how many of them had finished up in his dustpan.

He had an uncomfortable feeling that it had been rather a lot.

Infiltrate. Well, that should be easy enough.

'We go through the trap door?' he asked.

'Normally we would, but . . .'

'. . . It's, uh, blocked.'

'Blocked?' squeaked Muddlespot.

You couldn't *block* the trap door. You could lock it, weigh it down, sit over it armed with fiery swords and that, but there had to be a way of getting through. That was the point.

'We've tried it. The whole upper shaft is blocked. To a depth of about fifty fathoms.'

'What with?'

'We *think* it's pure diamond. No way through it. To get into her head, we have to do it the hard way – to Earth first, and then in through an eye or ear, without the subject realizing it's us.'

'Insinuation, we call it,' said the other guard.

'And the – er – Sleepless Watch?' Muddlespot ventured timidly. He had heard that bit and hadn't liked it at all. He knew what it meant. It meant the Enemy. It meant angels.

Angels were not called 'angels' in Pandemonium. The messages that came up from Low Command gave them names such as 'The Unenlightened', 'The Accursed', 'The Braindead' or 'The People Who Have *Really* Got It Coming'. But the rank and file – the guys

who had to go up there and meet them face to face –
just called them 'The Fluffies' and shot on sight.

Muddlespot had never met an angel and he didn't
want to. He saw them occasionally in the carvings on
the palace walls and that was already quite enough.
They were stern-eyed figures with wings, carrying
lances of lightning and swords of fire that looked every
bit as dangerous as Corozin's brass hammer. (Some of
their harps and trumpets looked pretty dangerous too.)

The palace carvings, of course, always showed the
angels getting the worst of things. In fact, some
of the most humorous scenes featured large numbers of
angels very much on the receiving end. Muddlespot
was not fooled. He thought about those trumpets and
wondered how he could possibly duck a hail of B flats.

He probably wouldn't even hear them coming.

'You'll, er, take care of them for me?' he pleaded.

'Death to the Fluffies,' intoned one guard.

The other held out a claw. A small pile of little
black spherical objects appeared in his talons. 'Your
tar bombs, Agent Muddlespot. Guaranteed to stick a
Fluffy's feathers when used at close range.'

'Your pitchfork,' said the first guard, producing one.
'To operate, grip firmly and thrust. In the right hands it
will pierce the heavenliest of heavenly armour.'

Muddlespot looked at his hands.

'Your communications set: dish, powder, matches . . . Use to report success only.'

'Pentagram, five-point, summoning for the use of—'

'Runes, mystic, casting for the use of—'

'Furnace, No. 19 portable—'

'Standard Disguise Set: Handsome Stranger, Fellow Traveller, Suave Gentleman—'

'Enhanced Disguise Set: Headmaster, Web Pal, Stand-Up Comedian—'

'Don't use the Headmaster – his cover's been blown—'

'And your Battle Manual, edition MCCCLXXVIII, latest issue from Low Command.' Both guards saluted.

The Battle Manual was a huge book, bound in black marble with brass fittings and pages of silky-smooth leather, or possibly human skin. It was four times the size of Muddlespot himself and creaked evilly when the guards rested it against the pile of other equipment that had suddenly accumulated in that little room. In the black marble burned letters of fire. They read: *How to Tempt.*

'Um . . .' said Agent Muddlespot, eyeing the teetering pile of equipment.

All right. He probably *could* carry it all. Carrying was just a matter of quantity, and quantity isn't the same in Pandemonium. But how was he going to keep it all sorted? How would he remember, in an emergency, what did what? He could just see himself reaching for a tar bomb and pulling out the furnace instead. A well-aimed furnace might pack more punch than an angelic piccolo, but there was no way it was going to beat one on the draw. He'd have been happier if they had just handed him a nice brass dustpan and brush.

'Synchronize watches,' intoned one guard, adjusting a large timepiece that had just appeared attached to his wrist.

'Mars is in Sagittarius . . .' replied the other, doing the same.

'Er – should I have a watch too?' asked Muddle-spot.

He had a sudden sinking feeling that time was running out.

He was right.

'Are you ready?'

'Er . . .'

'Then let's GO! Let's GO!'

5: INSINUATION

At the end of the corridor was a narrow flight of stairs. Up these stairs Muddlespot ran, with the guards urging him on from before and behind. His kit was in his sack and the sack was on his shoulder, and his tongue was hanging out with the effort of moving it all so far and so fast. Things scuttled in the shadows and whipped out of sight as he passed. Carved faces screamed at him silently. Up he ran, six flights, from the very bottom of the palace to the roof that looked out over the spires of Pandemonium.

Here on the flat terrace was a flying machine, built of batskin stretched over a frame that might have been mere wood but was probably bone. It was a twisted, lopsided, slithery thing, like a huge insect that had fallen in someone's bath and then been hit with the soap. By the time Muddlespot hauled himself out onto the roof, the leading guard had already put on some goggles and a flying scarf and was swinging the propeller. The machine buzzed sickeningly into life.

'Chocks away!' roared the guards, as they bundled into the cockpit.

Of course it was Muddlespot who had to pull the little horn-shaped chocks away from the wheels, and then run after the machine, which had started to canter across the roof terrace, and pile both himself and his kit sack into the back seat – where, it turned out, there was no seat, let alone a seatbelt or life jacket or nice smiling person telling him how to fasten one and blow the whistle on the other. (Corozin was, in fact, a fairly minor figure in Pandemonium, and his private airline was as basic as they came.)

The nose lifted. The rooftop dropped away beneath them. They soared out over the gulf of Pandemonium. All the brass spires pointed up towards them like the trunks of slender conifers on a mountainside ablaze. Before them was darkness, and into the darkness they steered, on and on.

The distant glow from the city behind them reflected on something ahead. It was a gate, with nine doors made of iron and brass and adamantine rock. It grew as they flew towards it.

It grew and grew, until it seemed the size of a small mountain and wide enough for an army of giants to march out in line abreast. Muddlespot went from wondering who was going to open it for them to wondering if there was really anyone anywhere who was big enough to open it at all.

Still it grew, huge, blank, impenetrable, and now Muddlespot saw that the whole adventure was going to end right there. Because, plainly, and whatever the guards and even Corozin might say, that gate just wasn't going to open for them.

It didn't open. It went on growing until the rivets were the size of hillocks and the nearest keyhole was like the mouth of a huge cave, yawning wider and wider as if to swallow them . . .

And it did. They flew through the keyhole with the guards whooping and cackling like children in a tunnel. Their voices echoed round the iron chamber and struck sparks from the metal. Then they were out into the wild abyss beyond, which was made of heat and cold and wet and dry, and was torn by great winds that tossed their craft to and fro and up and down, until Muddlespot's eyes bobbled in his head and he began to feel very uncomfortable indeed.

And on they flew. And on. Until the clouds parted, and they were skimming over the rooftops of Darlington Row.

'Alert!' cried an angel, high on a crystal tower. A thousand amber eyes opened.

(That was his watch mate, waking up. Angels are not challenged in the eye department. They can have as many as they need. A watch angel needs quite a lot of them.)

Together they looked at the scene below. They called the Seraph. In an instant he was with them. All along the watchtowers a shudder ran – the militant rustle of a million soft white feathers. Something was happening.

Cold-eyed, lean-jawed, the Seraph brooded like a thundercloud. He uttered a single word. 'Scramble!'

Golden trumpets blew. Flights of doves exploded from the towers like thistledown in a wind. They banked, one squadron after another, and swooped down upon Earth. Over the air came a message, loud and clear:'*Enemy craft approaching the Darlington Sector. Intercept and destroy!*'

There it was, a dark and clumsy insect, chugging steadily across the skies to the very heart of the High Security Zone. A sitting target.

The squadrons banked in pursuit.

Muddlespot was struggling into a parachute that the guards had passed back to him. It was the act of shrugging the awkward thing onto his shoulders that made him tilt his head back and lift his eyes to the sky – the sky of white, puffy clouds that now, suddenly, seemed to be speckling with little black dots. Little black *fast-moving* dots.

He gaped at them for a moment. Then he let out a shriek.

One of the guards looked up. 'Doves at six o'clock high!' he cried. 'Evasive action!'

The hell-plane flipped onto its side and dropped like a stone. Pursued by the threatening coos of enraged doves, it zigzagged desperately over the neat front gardens of Darlington Row. The air hissed. Little white missiles showered all around them. Three landed in a row within inches of Muddlespot's nose, and burned a neat line of holes in the bat skin. The holes smoked at the edges.

'Aaahahaahah!' cried a guard in terror, as the plane

54

flung itself to the right and the first dove squadron peeled away.

'Five o'clock! Five o'clock!' cried his fellow.

'And three and seven and eight o'clock!' screamed Muddlespot, who had taken the time to look around.

In they came, merciless, swooping out of the sun . . .

And you can weave and spin, you can dive and climb and do Immelmann turns, but there's no evading the doves. You can run, but they're faster than you are. And you can't hide. They get you whatever you do. They get you every time.

(Just ask anyone who owns a car.)

In they came. Again the sky hissed. Little piles of dove poo splattered on the wings. The engine coughed. A sulphurous fume flew back from the cowling and blinded Muddlespot where he sat. The attacking squadron banked away but others were still pursuing. The sky was full of enemies, swift, implacable and armed to the anus.

'Target ahead!' cried one of the guards.

Trailing a stream of yellow smoke, the machine shot through an open window. Muddlespot, peering fearfully from his seat, looked out on a landscape of carpet and tablecloth and doorways and cat bowls all reeling backwards beneath him.

'Get ready to jump!'

Everything was spinning. Now, what was beneath him was an upside-down lamp and shade sprouting from a very upside-down ceiling. And above him, also upside down, drifted the face of Sally Jones, huge, saying something like *'Let me do that for you.'*

'Jump, Muddlespot! Jump!' screamed a guard as everything righted itself.

'Um – I've got this sudden pain!' wailed Muddlespot.

'Send us a card about it! JUMP!'

'But I don't want to die!'

A long, leathery arm reached back from the cockpit and grabbed him by the neck. *'Sure* you do!' the guard cried. And hurled him out into space.

Air rushing . . .

Insides wriggling in terror . . .

Which way is up?

A moment ago, *that* was . . .

A chaos of light, and of unfamiliar things, spinning before his eyes . . .

And some of it is getting horribly nearer, horribly quickly . . .

The air is bellowing in his ears . . .

WHACK!

Miraculously, the parachute had opened above him. The canopy billowed into a beautiful, comforting half-sphere, with a pair of jaunty slit eyes and horns blazoned on the middle of it. Somewhere above him the wounded machine flew on, its engine coughing and its smoke-trail thickening. The ground was swaying up to meet him, but no longer rushing as if to crush him to pulp. He had time to look around, to try to understand this place that was to be his field of action, and that he had never seen before.

The smells hit him immediately. They were strong and unfamiliar. Soap scum, leather, carpet dust and old cat – he knew none of them. He recognized the scent of an oven (there were quite a lot of ovens in Pandemonium), but the sweet, moist overlay was totally new to him. He knew nothing about baking. Ovens were for meat – preferably meat that was still living. Dough was to Muddlespot as sunspots would be to an Amazonian slug. It just did not compute.

The room itself seemed to him to be a huge, cubical cavern with pale walls and a floor the size of an ocean. Except that he knew it couldn't really be an ocean, not here. For one thing, it was blue. (There isn't much blue in Pandemonium, and what there is doesn't appear in the oceans, which are mostly cooking fat.) There were rectangular shapes on the walls. He did not realize, then, that some of these shapes were pictures and others were windows, or that there was any difference between the two.

The chaotic profusion of objects bewildered him. The house contained all the furniture and possessions of two working adults and two teenagers, including office papers, newspapers, bills, sports kits, school kits, a cat, a largely forgotten tidying rota and nowhere to put the boots. Stuff was everywhere.

And it was all *huge*. It was far larger than he had imagined it would be. When he looked down again he saw that he was about to make his landing on what appeared to be a mountain covered with dark forest. He waggled his arms and legs a bit to see if he could steer, and found he couldn't.

He was still clutching his equipment sack. His mind had forgotten all about that in his terror, but his hand hadn't. Or maybe it had just forgotten to let go. He dropped it now, letting it fall the last few fathoms to the ground, and gathered himself to land as lightly and gracefully as he could in this new world.

THUMP!

Winded, groaning, Muddlespot got to his hands and knees. He untangled himself from the strings of his parachute, took the bag off his back and stuffed as much of the canopy as he could back into it. He limped over to where his kit lay, found various bits that had fallen out of the sack and stuffed them away too. Then he straightened and looked at the forest around him.

It wasn't a forest of trees. (There *are* trees in Pandemonium. They make them of brass.)

These were a bit like trees, to be sure. They seemed to be about the thickness of slender young saplings. But they had no branches. And after rising several times his height from the ground, they bent over and lay one on top of another, all in one direction as if shaped by some terrific wind.

With a creeping feeling in his stomach, Muddlespot realized that they were human hairs. And very probably, unless the guards had made some enormous mistake, they were part of Sally Jones. He was standing on her head, and her head was – to him – the size of a mountain.

Muddlespot was used to being smaller than everything else. But that was because Corozin had chosen that he should be. Corozin could make anything he had power over be any size he liked. If Corozin had chosen that his palace cleaner should be a hundred fathoms tall, then that's how it would have been. (Muddlespot would have rather liked being the only hundred-fathom-high former wart in existence. It would have made dusting the palace spires *so* much easier.)

But here on Earth, Quantity ruled. Quantity said that things like Muddlespot were Ideas. Ideas had to be small. It didn't matter how big an Idea they were, said Quantity. They could be Freedom or Liberty or World Peace for all Quantity cared. But they still had to fit inside a head without causing too much discomfort to the head's owner.

It's true that some Ideas kicked back against this. They were Really Big Ideas, they said. They knew things about Quantity that made Quantity look like it wore nappies. No way were *they* going to be told how much space they fitted into. The Theories of Relativity bent space, warped time, predicted black holes and singularities and chucked in a cosmological constant just to show what they thought of Quantity. But all it got them was enough room to make their owner's hair stand on end.

So there was Muddlespot, tiny, smaller than a fleck of skin, abandoned in the vast forest that was the scalp of Sally Jones.

And the light around him grew.

Someone behind him said '*Freeze.*'

6: THE MIND OF SALLY JONES

The angel towered over him. It might have been carved from bright marble or shining steel. Or very, very hard light. Muddlespot had to squint at it to see.

It was all straight lines – head, wings, feet. Its dark glasses were rectangles. Its tuxedo was pressed in crisp white lines, its little black bow tie was a cubist's dream. Even its fiery hair flamed in little zigzags. In its rock-steady hands it gripped a great bassoon, with the mouth pointed right between Muddlespot's eyes.

Muddlespot's hands shot up as high as they could – which was just slightly below the level of his ears.

'Well, well, well,' said the angel, in tones like bells tuned in C sharp. 'What have we here?'

'Er . . .' said Muddlespot. He thought of various

possible answers. None of them seemed likely to improve things. 'Is there time to defect?'

'Nice try, creep,' said the angel, 'but I don't think so.' It spoke into a mouthpiece. 'Hello, base? I have the intruder. Shall I purify?'

'Mercy!' cried Muddlespot, throwing himself forward and grovelling among his scattered kit. 'I'm too young to die!'

'*You have your orders, Blue Two*,' said a voice from midair. '*Yay, verily*.'

'Too bad, creep,' said the angel, hefting the bassoon. 'Say your prayers. Oh, I forgot – you people don't, do you? Just say "Goodbye" then.'

Muddlespot's little claw, clutching frantically, closed on the thing he was looking for. 'Goodbye!' he squeaked. And he rolled, and threw it at the angel's feet. *SPLOTCH!* went the tar bomb in a fountain of black ickiness. The light was smothered at once.

The angel was blinded, covered head to foot in black goo – and *very* angry. It wiped its eyes on its sleeve. The bassoon quested from left to right. Just let that little creep show himself and he'd get blasted so hard he'd still be travelling outwards when all the galaxies collided!

But Muddlespot was gone. All that was left was an

abandoned No. 19 portable furnace, a few scattered runes and a frantic scurrying somewhere in the under-growth.

'Base!' yelled the angel. 'I've lost him! Request urgent backup!'

'ALERT! ALERT! ALERT!' sang angel choirs in close polyphony. Rainbow gates clanged open. Steeds of fire trampled. Saints shook their lances and hurried out to battle. The air rang with alarums. 'ALERT! ALERT! YAY, VERILY ALERT!'

Fierce-eyed robins established a cordon in the bushes around the Jones household. Shock troops equipped with cymbals, harps, triangles and trumpets moved in behind a creeping barrage laid down by an organ in the old mission hall, while low-hovering afreets and pegasi circled in support.

But Muddlespot was ahead of them. He was already tumbling into space, hanging by an abseil line from the tip of Sally's ear. Down, down he went, burning his hands in his hurry, kicking out with his little feet so that he could swing inwards on the return, and release, and fall in a heap in the delicate curled canyons of Sally's auricle. There he lay breathless, listening to the clamour of the hunt and the growing clatter of feet in corridors nearby.

Voices called. Wings rushed. Muddlespot cowered in his place as troops of security angels poured past him, hurrying out from their posts in Sally's brain to scour the slopes of her shoulders for signs of the intruder.

The sounds faded. He waited. No more came.

After a long while he picked himself up, gathered his considerably reduced kit sack, and began to softly make his way in the direction from which they had come.

Upwards.

Inwards.

Into the mind of Sally Jones.

There was a high archway, carried on slender pillars. Beyond was a six-sided chamber. On each side of it was an arch like the first, opening onto long corridors of diminishing perspectives, or onto flights of broad steps leading either up or down. A gallery ran around the chamber, far above Muddlespot's head. More arches opened from it, one after another. The archways were not round or pointed but parabola, intersecting at the ceiling with an ordered complexity that could only have been conceived by someone who really *liked* that sort of maths.

Everything was made of glass, or some transparent crystal. He could see through walls and through floors, to other chambers and corridors far above his head, or many, many levels below his feet. It was dizzying. It made him feel that the floor was about to give way and send him tumbling through layer after layer of thought. Some of the surfaces were plain; others were patterned with complex translucent designs like mosaics of stars or unicorns rising from waves. These broke up the passage of light, discreetly concealing whatever lay beyond them. In a corridor a level below this one was a row of doors. Muddlespot could just make out the lettering on some of them. FRENCH SUBJUNCTIVE, one said. And next to that was DECLENSION OF IRREGULAR FRENCH VERBS.

The corridor stretched on and on to the left and right. There must have been a thousand doors of it. And beyond it was another, and another, and . . .

Music seemed to be playing somewhere, but he couldn't catch what it was or which direction it came from.

'*Un*usual,' he murmured to himself.

He had thought that the mind of a schoolgirl would be a rather small place. He had imagined that there would be bright colours and childish pictures, and lots of things like bowling alleys and swings and slides. He had been rather looking forward to the slides.

'*Unusual, unusual*,' echoed the crystal passages, as

if they agreed with him and were also a little proud of it. They spread in all directions, intricate and yet ordered. Everything had symmetry. Every feature had its mirror image. There was no dust. There was no movement. There was no sound of voices. There were a million ideas in Sally's head, but they didn't go wandering about. They stayed in their rooms until they were wanted. And when they were wanted, they had to move quickly.

Feeling very small, Muddlespot climbed a flight of broad stairs to reach another chamber. There was a crystal figure in the middle of it. A graceful torso rose from a block of sculpted ice. The head was a man's, with a full beard. He was crowned with leaves. Blank-eyed, he gazed along his outstretched, smoothly muscled arm. His index finger pointed to one of the chamber's six arches. Above the arch was written in words of gold, LOOK FOR THE RIGHT.

'The right,' grumbled Muddlespot nervously. 'Yeah, yeah, right.' But he went the way that he was pointed. It led down another long corridor and past a court where a fountain was playing. He crossed the open space quickly. On the far side was a higher, wider arch and above it, again in gold letters, were the words IT IS BETTER TO GIVE THAN TO RECEIVE.

'I don't believe it,' muttered Muddlespot.

And: 'She *can't* be for real!'

In their niches, statues brooded silently. Their blank eyes looked down on him. *Oh yes she can*, they seemed to say. *Yes she can.*

There was another flight of stairs, as wide as a basketball court and very long. Muddlespot panted up it, hurrying because he knew there couldn't be much time before the squadrons of angels he had seen leaving earlier gave up their search and returned to their posts. At the top was another arch. Beyond it was a chamber. This was the place.

The ceiling was set with stars. A pantheon of crystal statues, marked with names such as TRUTH, WISDOM, FAIRNESS and CALM, stood in a semi-circle around the centre of the room. And opposite, curving round the far wall, were two huge arched windows. The windows looked out onto the world in which Sally lived. He saw the room that had spun before his eyes during his desperate flight and jump. He saw a formica tabletop, on which were laid text-books, calculators, neatly ordered pens and a workbook on which Sally's own hand was writing, in beautiful, round letters, the words *Essay on the Fall of Roman Civilization in Britain.*

Sally had finished making the dough, had stood guard over the oven while it meekly did what she wanted, and had turned out two dozen flawless small cakes onto the cooling rack. Now she was doing her homework. She had everything she needed. She had pen, paper, essay plan and the cat curled up in her lap. (The cat wasn't really needed for the homework, but he had got so much into the habit of jumping up into her lap when he saw her sitting down with pen and paper that somehow it would have felt wrong to start without him. Sally thought he was hopelessly selfish, but she had a soft spot for him all the same because at least he was honest about it.)

And here, in the high inner chamber of her mind, set within the semicircle of statues, there was another table, exactly like the one Muddlespot could see through the window. It was set with the same books. The same pencils and calculators were laid out upon it. And seated in a chair, cat in lap and head bowed over her writing, was another Sally.

The Sally. The central idea of Sally. The Sally who always would be Sally, no matter what changes happened to her in the outside world. The person who had made this mind of arches and statues and golden letters what it was.

Muddlespot wouldn't have been surprised to find that the Inner Sally had a head the size of a beach ball – or possibly a small planet. But she didn't.

He wouldn't have been *that* surprised if he had found that the Inner Sally was a fierce little woman about a hundred and fifty years old, with sharp eyes and a face that only ever smiled when the very last grain of dust had been swept off her floor. She wasn't.

He wouldn't have been totally astonished to find that she was really a fire-breathing dragon. She wasn't.

The Sally he saw here looked exactly the same as her outer self. Which should have meant that she was entirely happy with the way she was.

But there was just one little difference.

Her ankles were tied fast to the chair. Round her waist ran loop after loop of rope, pulled so tight that it must have been horribly uncomfortable. Her arms were free, but only so that she could turn pages and write things. Her mouth was stopped with a great white gag, and muffs were clamped fast over her ears.

Muddlespot squeaked with dismay.

She did not see him coming because she was intent on the page. She did not hear him because of the muffs. Only when he reached her and started tugging at the knotted ropes did she realize he was there. She turned her head to him.

'Mmmm! Mmmm! Mmmm!' she said through her gag.

'Coming!' gasped Muddlespot. 'Won't be a moment!'

The knots were very tight.

'Mmmm! Mmmm! Mmmm!'

'Just as . . . soon as I can!' said Muddlespot, working frantically. 'There!'

'*Mmmm! Mmmm! Mmmm!*'

'Oh, sorry!' He pulled the earmuffs away and loosened the gag. It dropped to her neck.

'WHAT ARE YOU DOING?!?' yelled Sally.

'I . . . er . . . freeing you?'

'And who *asked* you?' She rose to her feet. She towered over him like an emperor over some poor subject. This lasted for half a second before her ankles, still tied to the chair, tripped her up and she had to sit down with a bump. The chair teetered, tipped and sent her sprawling.

Muddlespot scratched his head. The gag in his hand was definitely a gag. It didn't look at all nice to wear. He couldn't think of any reason why anyone would want one. But it was dawning on him that (however odd and crazy it seemed) things were the way they were inside the human mind for a reason. And the reason was that humans really did like their minds to be that way. They had got used to it. Maybe they couldn't think of anything better. Anyway, they weren't going to thank anyone who just came along and changed them.

'I didn't know you had to ask,' he said lamely.

'See?' said Sally, righting herself awkwardly. 'You come in here, thinking you know best . . . What did you want, anyway?'

What did he want? Muddlespot focused on the question.

Ah. Yes. And he'd better get on with it – before the Sleepless Watch came back to their bunks.

'Ahem! Do I have your full attention?'

'You've as much as you're going to get,' she said. 'And it'll be less every second.'

He took a deep breath. 'I'm here to get you to come over to *our* side,' he said, with as much confidence as he could muster.

She looked at him thoughtfully. 'And how will you do that?'

'By offering you all the nations of the Earth.' Out of his sack he pulled a long, long scroll of what might have been cured skin, written with many comforting-looking mystic spiky characters in ink that might have been distilled from molten bone marrow. 'All you have to do is bow down and worship me. Sign here, please.'

Sally gave him another thoughtful look. One of her eyebrows lifted slightly, as if she detected that his origins might have been a bit on the warty side. 'Could I worship Johnny Depp instead?' she asked.

Muddlespot hesitated. 'Er . . . that might be all right. Let me check.'

Out came the book bound in black marble, followed by sounds of frantic rustling as Muddlespot searched for guidance.

'Forget it,' sighed Sally. 'I'm not interested.'

'What about wealth?' asked Muddlespot hurriedly, still leafing through his book.

'No.'

'Fame?'

'No.'

'Beauty?'

The eyebrows lifted again – just a little.

So much can be said in just a little.

'I mean – I mean *amazing* beauty,' gabbled Muddlespot. 'Beauty *even* more beautiful than you've got now. You know – crack-the-glass sort of beauty . . . um . . . What about it?'

'You can't take a hint, can you?'

'Apple?' said Muddlespot, producing one.

'No thanks.'

'Don't you want *anything*?' cried Muddlespot desperately.

'I want you to tie me up again,' said Sally, holding out her bonds. 'Get to it.'

'Tie you up? You *want* to be tied up?'

'I'm good with it. Keeps me focused.'

'No – hang on. This can't be right . . .'

'It's *my* mind, isn't it?'

'But—'

'DO IT!'

Hands trembling, Muddlespot began to wind the bonds around her. He was thinking, I shouldn't be doing this. I'm letting her win. I should be saying something, talking her over . . . Corozin will spread me all over his ceiling if he hears about this . . . I've got to say *something*. Even if it's only . . .

'Er . . . how's that?'

'Tighter,' growled Sally, picking up her pen.

And Sally was thinking, There's no time for this. To get the History essay done properly was going to take another hour. Then there would be dinner, and after dinner a chance to put in half an hour on next week's Physics homework, do some reading (*Paradise*

Lost) and get all her things ready for tomorrow. Mustn't forget that washing-up too . . .

Cheek! Coming in here and starting to chat her up when she was already busy! And dumb. What had he *thought* she was going to say?

Quite cute though. That air of helpless bewilderment made her want to pat him on the head and say, 'There, there, don't mind so much. You'll be better at this when you've had – er – quite a lot of practice . . .'

He was still fumbling with her bonds. She wished he would hurry up. For his sake as well as hers. It couldn't be long before the . . .

'THERE HE IS!'

'BLAST HIM!'

'DON'T LET HIM GET AWAY!'

. . . guards came back.

7: IN A CAT DISH

A strange murmur filtered down crystal corridors. Beneath the arches the air trembled. The music wavered. In their alcoves and on their plinths, the heads of blank-eyed statues bent to listen. It was a sound they had not heard in a long, long while.

The mind of Sally Jones was undergoing a mild disturbance.

'THERE HE GOES!'

(Mild, but nevertheless unusual.)

'*Gold fifteen! Intruder is on the stairs! Cut him off!*'

'DIE, scum! Yay verily!'

Muddlespot flung himself over a balustrade, skidded round a corner and frantically reversed direction at the sight of four more angels advancing, instruments in hand. He dived for cover behind a plinth. Trumpets blew and trombones blasted. The notes sang past his ears and wrote themselves in little quartets all over the wall behind him. He threw a tar bomb and didn't stop to see where it went.

Down another corridor, feet pounding, pursued by cries. The six-sided chamber with the pointing statue. The exit ahead of him . . .

Angels in the gallery above!

Something small, hurtling through the air!

BANG!

Ears ringing, Muddlespot skittered sideways. The air was full of a horribly sweet-smelling smoke. It stung his skin. He pounded on down the last corridor. The way out into the world was ahead of him. From behind came the sounds of rushing wings and running feet, and cries of '*He's getting away!*' (which sounded good) and '*Don't miss!*' (which didn't sound good at all). He groped in his sack for another tar bomb. There weren't any.

He found the trident, which might have worked at close range, except that right now close range was very much where he didn't want to be . . .

He found the parachute, which he had stuffed back in his sack earlier . . .

He ran out of Sally's ear canal like he was running full tilt out of a cave in a mountainside . . .

He was falling, the air rushing up past him. He was shaking the parachute desperately with one hand . . .

And *WHACK!* For a second time the parachute opened into a beautiful, comforting curve above his head. His mad descent seemed to stop in midair. 'So long, suckers!' he called cheerfully to the angels who crowded at the lip of Sally's ear, pointing arms and weapons down at him.

TARATARATARATARATTARATAAAA! went the trumpets above him. Golden notes flew through his canopy and ripped it to shreds. Muddlespot's eyes bulged in terror.

Then he was falling again.

He fell a long way.

A long, long way.

And the ground rushed up to meet him. And it went on rushing, expanding madly as he got closer and closer and closer to it until . . .

SPLAT!

'Ooo-ooh!' groaned a dazed Muddlespot.

'Muddlespot?' said a voice he knew, somewhere nearby. It wasn't one he particularly wanted to hear.

'Muddlespot? Are you receiving me?'

Muddlespot opened his eyes. He was lying on his back in a heap of brown goo, surrounded by what seemed to be a smooth silver wall that rose up in a circle all around him. Looking down on him out of the sky was a huge face.

It was round and covered in black hair. It was topped with two huge triangular ears. Its mouth was a short, straight line that looked as if, when it opened, it could open very wide indeed and be full of red tongue and sharp white teeth. It had a small black button nose that twitched suspiciously, and two huge yellow eyes with slit pupils that peered down upon him as if trying to make out what he was.

(Shades, the Jones household cat, lived by a few very simple rules. One was 'Dinnertime Is Anytime'. The following scene will illustrate . . .

SHADES:	*Miaaoooww?*
SALLY:	You've been fed, Shades.
SHADES:	*Miaaoooww?*
SALLY:	You've been fed, Shades.

SHADES:	*Miaaoooww?*
SALLY:	You've been fed, Shades.
SHADES:	*Miaaoooww?*
SALLY:	Shut up and let me do my homework!
SHADES:	*Miaaoooww?*
SALLY:	What's the matter with you? There's still a mountain of stuff in your bowl!

This replays itself hourly in the Jones household, with minor variations but only one ending – the arrival of a fresh helping of cat food, with a layer of nice gleaming fresh jelly, in Shades's dish. There is no other way it can possibly go. Sally knows Shades is a greedy, selfish, heartless professional beggar. But Shades knows a softie when he sees one.)

Now, if you *are* going to fall off the side of a mountain and into someone's cat dish, the one thing that might save you from serious harm is a layer of nice fresh jelly. So it was lucky for Muddlespot that he had made his landing in the crucial few seconds between Sally opening the new tin and Shades's swift arrival for Third Supper.

Another of Shades's rules – and this too worked in Muddlespot's favour – was 'Never Eat Anything You

Think Might Have Something In It'. It was shocking, what the family tried to hide in his food sometimes: namely vitamins, more vitamins and worming tablets. Shades strongly disliked worming tablets. It was not just that they tasted foul. He thought they made life too easy for his humans.

And this time there *was* something in his bowl. It did not look like a worming tablet, ground up into powder. It did not smell like a worming tablet either. It smelled very largely of cat food, but with lingering traces of other things. Not bad as such (after that near miss with the incense bomb, Muddlespot probably smelled better than he ever had in his life). But Shades had not got where he was by being broad-minded. If it was In His Food, then he was Not Having It. He turned away from the cat dish and stalked off in disgust, leaving a perfectly good third supper untouched as a mark of his affront.

'Muddlespot!' came Corozin's voice again. 'Why don't you answer?'

It was coming from inside his sack.

Still groaning, Muddlespot dragged himself and the remnants of his equipment to firmer ground. There he tipped out the contents of the sack and found the communications dish. It had somehow already filled itself with powder, and the powder was glowing a lively yellow-green. Within the glow was a pair of eyes that Muddlespot knew well.

'Muddlespot?' said Corozin. 'Why have you not reported success?'

'Er . . .' said Muddlespot. He wondered if there was any good way of saying what he had to say.

There wasn't.

Heaven and Hell are opposites. There is no meeting place, no middle ground, no possible compromise between them. There is no way that they can be likened to one another, brought together, put in the same box or even encompassed in the same thought. They are black and white, night and day, matter and antimatter or whatever the other stuff is. In the Long War, there is no peace. There simply cannot be.

And yet, both are organizations. Both have people who are bossed and people who do the bossing. And bosses everywhere are a bit the same. *Especially* when they somehow weren't around when whatever it was that happened happened. And they get to tell you what *would* have happened if only they'd been there to do it themselves . . .

'You WHAAAAAT?'

cried the Seraph. Before him the ranks of security angels quailed. Little beads of sweat stood out on their foreheads like gems glistening on silk.

'This is FAILURE!'

screamed the Seraph, and his voice cracked the pillars of air and shook the arches of the palaces above the clouds.

'Betrayal! Dereliction of duty! She is our *top priority* subject in the whole of Darlington Row. There were a *legion* of you, and just one of the Enemy. And you allowed him to *infiltrate*? To speak with her? To escape without capture? Do you call *this* security?'

'You WHAAAAAT?'

cried Corozin. Before the fiery eyes in his communications dish, poor Muddlespot trembled. So did the jelly he was coated in.

'This is FAILURE!'

screamed Corozin, and his voice rang around his brass palace, and caused quite a stir in the cat dish too.

'Betrayal! Dereliction of duty! She is our *top priority* subject in the whole of Darlington Row. We *got* you all the way there, Muddlespot. Past all the doves and guards and wards of the Enemy. And you *didn't* secure a defection? Do you call *this* success?'

The agents of Pandemonium, however, do have one advantage. They may let Truth take second place to Self-Preservation. Across the cat dish floated the words, 'But she *liked* me, Your Serenity.'

Muddlespot heard them but only with difficulty, because his ears were being scorched and blasted by the displeasure of Corozin, and because a long demonic arm (with *perfectly* beautiful fingernails) had magically reached out of the pile of glowing powder, caught him by the neck and was shaking him up and down until his sight darkened and his mind was swimming in the final cloud.

But hear them he did. And gasping, he managed to repeat them. 'Buff – ee – ike – me – Ur – Fferen-enenenefy!'

The shaking stopped. Muddlespot dangled in the air. The beautifully manicured nails dug deep into his neck.

'What did you say?'

'She asked me to call again,' said the voice softly.

'Fee afk ee mo 'all a'ain,' said Muddlespot, whose ability to speak was still compromised by the pressure of a giant (but very beautiful) thumb across most of his face.

'That's *better*! Why didn't you say so?' The

demonic arm lowered him gently and set him on his feet.

'I got a date and a number, boss,' said the voice.

'I got . . .' began Muddlespot.

'Thank you, but I heard it the first time. And it's "*Serenity*", Muddlespot. Se-*rehnity*. Not "boss". I cannot abide "boss". It is vulgar. Is that clear?'

'Yes, Your Ser-ee-ee-nity!' squeaked Muddlespot, and bowed.

One elegant, purple-nailed finger jabbed him on the nose. 'See here, Muddlespot. I like you. I expect great things of you. You're like a son to me, etcetera. But Low Command is on my back. They want this kid taken care of. If we disappoint them, I'm for the ovens. And then where will you be?'

'Yes, Your Serenity,' said Muddlespot, bobbing and squeaking like a rusty yo-yo.

'Don't fail me.'

The arm and the eyes vanished. The glow faded. From nowhere, it seemed, a faint draught blew across the communications dish, lifting the smouldering powder in a fine smoke and dispersing it into the air.

'Narrow escape there, kid,' said the voice.

'Yes,' gasped Muddlespot, who was trying to stop

his teeth chattering by clamping his hands one to either side of his jaw. It wasn't working very well. 'Who – who are you anyway?' he added.

'Thought you'd never ask.'

There he was, leaning nonchalantly against a lump of drying cat food. He was almost the colour of cat food himself.

'The name's *Scattletail*,' he said.

8: SCATTLETAIL

He was the smallest, shabbiest, evillest-looking creature Muddlespot had ever seen. His eyes were bright black little horizontal slits. His nose was twice the length of his head, curving and pointed like the beak of some wading bird. He wore a battered broad-brimmed hat the same brown colour as his skin, and a shapeless, rumpled coat that covered him from his lips all the way down to his toes. His mouth was tiny and sloped a little to one side, as if all the talking he ever did was done sideways.

'You're one of us?' asked Muddlespot, knowing it must be true but not quite believing it.

'Strictly speaking, kid. Strictly speaking.' The words came out of the side of Scattletail's mouth, just as Muddlespot had suspected. 'I'm assigned to Billie there.' He jerked his thumb over his shoulder.

Muddlespot looked up.

And up.

From down here, the huge forms of the humans were like clouds drifting in the sky. Yes, they were there. Yes, they were big. But it was impossible to say how big, how far away, or exactly what meaning they had down here at the level of cat spittle.

There seemed to be three of them now, gathered round the table. They were Sally, her mother and the blonde, dishevelled girl whom Muddlespot vaguely remembered was Sally's twin. Their voices filtered down to the cat dish like distant thunder.

'But I can't do my homework!' the blonde girl was screaming. 'She's got the pencil sharpener!'

'That's Sally's pencil sharpener, dear,' said Mrs Jones. She sounded as if she felt like screaming herself. 'So where's yours?'

'It's not hers! She stole it and put her name on it!'

'I put her name on it, Billie. I named hers and yours after the last time. Remember?'

'She can have the pencil sharpener,' said Sally.

'Thank you, Sally,' said Mum. 'Now, Billie—'

'I need the calculator too!' said Billie crossly, and snatched at it.

'But that's Sally's . . .'

'She can have the calculator,' said Sally.

'Right,' said Billie. 'And I need quiet too! So you have to stop her from doing violin practice until I've finished. I'm already late starting because of her, and I won't be able to get it all done in time and I'll have to hand it in late again and I'll probably get punished and I'll get a bad report and it'll be all her fault. AGAIN!'

'I've done my violin practice,' said Sally.

BANG-rattle! Billie had somehow bumped into the leg of the table, knocking Sally's glass of water over her carefully written page.

'That looks like an easy number,' said Muddlespot enviously.

SLAM!

went the door behind Billie.

'It is and it isn't,' said Scattletail.

STOMP! STOMP! STOMP! STOMP! STOMP! STOMP! STOMP! went Billie's feet on the stairs.

'I bet *she* hasn't got squadrons of Fluffies looking after her.'

SLAM! went Billie's bedroom door.

'You can tell, can you?' Scattletail lit a cigarette and put it into the corner of his mouth. (What with all his words *and* the cigarette, which was there most of the time, the left-hand corner of Scattletail's mouth had a lot to do. The rest of him made up for it by doing as little as possible.) 'Nope. She just has the standard detail. One guardian angel. Name of Ismael. He works hard, I'll give him that . . .' He blew a long puff of sulphurous yellow smoke. 'But most of the time I run rings around him.'

Obediently, the smoke became a ring of little Scattletails, running busily around the figure of an angel who sat dejectedly in the middle of the circle.

Muddlespot sat dejectedly in the middle of the cat dish. He looked at his toes. His ears drooped. He felt a lump forming in his throat and his eyesight was going misty.

'Sally's impossible,' he said forlornly.

Scattletail eyed him through narrow, dark, slitty eyes. 'Yeah?' he said.

'I tried everything! She wouldn't listen!'

'Still in one piece, ain't you?'

'Well, yes,' said Muddlespot, thinking gloomily of the piles beneath Corozin's windows. 'For the moment I am.'

'So what'd she say?'

'She's not interested,' said Muddlespot. His words thudded in his ears like a brass hammer falling. He clamped his mouth shut and put his chin on his hands. He thought he was going to cry.

'All right,' said Scattletail after a bit. 'What'd *you* say?'

'Everything I could. I promised her the lot: the nations, wealth, fame, beauty . . .'

'Everything that Low Command says, right?'

'Even the apple!'

Scattletail blew another puff of sulphurous smoke. He seemed to think for a moment. Then he sidled up to where Muddlespot sat. 'You use that book, *How to Tempt?*' he whispered.

'MCCCLXXVIIIth edition,' said Muddlespot tearfully.

'Feed the furnace with it.'

Muddlespot's ears drooped further. 'I lost the furnace,' he said.

'Doesn't matter. Dump the book. Get rid of it. It's just dead weight.'

'But then the Other Side will find it!'

'Better still.'

'Do you know what you're *saying?*'

Scattletail came closer. The waft of his breath made even Muddlespot gag. And his nose would have poked Muddlespot in the eye if he hadn't turned his head sideways. But Scattletail was always turning his head sideways. It meant he could use the corner of his mouth better. Under the battered brim of his hat his eyes were like a gunfighter's – a gunfighter who had seen a hundred fights and had survived them all.

'Corozin give you that thing?'

'Yes – well, his people did.'

Puff. (Gag.)

'Means they're more scared of Low Command than anything else. They give it to you, at least Low Command can't do them for the way they've briefed you. Corozin knows it doesn't work. But Low Command – not one of them's been up here for centuries. They think things up here are the same as they've always been. And things have changed. Things have changed lots.'

Puff. (Gag, yuck!) In the yellow fumes around Scattletail's head, more shapes were stirring. They were faces. A dozen Sallys opened their eyes. Twenty Billies spun slowly before Muddlespot's face. And there were more. Many, many more.

'Kids these days – they *know* things. More than Low Command dreams of. *Or* the Other Side, come to that. And what they don't know they don't need. Do they know a sell when they see one? You bet they do.'

'Right,' said Muddlespot, who was feeling ill.

'And does Low Command listen? Like stone walls, that's how they listen. "Kids are easy," they say. "Get 'em young," and all that.'

He spat. A great yellow blob went *whang-sizzlizzle!* as it hit the floor of the cat dish.

'Nope. Gimme a banker. A big-salary exec, just a couple of rungs off the top. Or a single working mum. Someone who's had a bit of time to get afraid. *They're* easy. But the kids . . .' He spat another blob of yellow. The Jones family didn't know it yet, but Shades wasn't going to want anything out of this bowl for a week.

'Right,' said Muddlespot. He got to his feet.

'Where're you goin'?'

'I'm going to report back down below,' said Muddlespot. 'And get spread all over the ceiling.'

'Shouldn't do that,' said Scattletail calmly.

'I thought it would save time.'

'Now look, kid—'

'Well, what's the *point*? How do I even start? She's under Sleepless Watch from about a million heavily armed Fluffies from On High! Her trap door's blocked with fifty fathoms of solid diamond! She even ties herself up in her own head!'

The little black eyes looked at him. 'Why?'

'What do you mean, why? That's what she's like – impregnable!'

'I mean, why does she want to be like that? What makes her tick? Must be something.'

Muddlespot frowned.

'Quite a lot of work, to be that tough,' Scattletail said. 'Not easy. Not fun, for a kid. So why? You find out, maybe you find something to work on. More you work on it, easier it gets. And go for the little things. Forget the "bow down and worship me". Little's what you want. Stuff they can tell themselves doesn't really matter. Then later' – he winked – 'you make sure it does, see?'

'I can't go in there again!' cried Muddlespot. 'There are guards all over the place!'

'Ye-es, but . . .' Scattletail sucked his cheeks. 'If you go *right now*, maybe you'll find they're all shooting each other.'

'Seriously?'

'Sure. 'S the problem with the Other Side – they've got high standards. You weren't supposed to have come within a mile of her.'

Muddlespot looked up. High above them loomed the figures of Sally and her mother, mopping up the water that Billie had spilled all over Sally's homework. Distantly the voices filtered down into the cat dish.

'She doesn't *mean* to be like this, Sally . . .'

'I know, Mum.'

'It's hard for her. At school and everything.'

'I know, Mum. Could I have another glass of water?'

'Of course, sweetheart . . .'

'This could be your best chance,' muttered Scattle-tail.

'Right,' sighed Muddlespot.

He thought about Sally. He thought about going back down and prostrating himself under Corozin's hammer.

Sally?

Hammer?

Sally.

Wearily, he picked up the remains of his gear. He pointed himself across the cat dish. He took one step. Then he took another.

'Oh, and kid,' said Scattletail behind him.

'Yes?'

'She's important, yeah?'

'Top Priority,' said Muddlespot, surprised at the question.

'Low Command's interested, right?'

'You bet they are.'

'Then, if you do get anywhere with her . . .'

'What?'

Scattletail's eyes flicked left and right, like little black fish in dark water. 'Then watch your back,' he whispered. 'Watch . . . Corozin.'

9: 'NO'

It's as good to travel as to arrive.

Muddlespot certainly found it so. And he had plenty of time to think about it because he had plenty of travelling to do. So long as he was travelling, no one was shooting at him and no one was hitting him with hammers. As soon as he arrived, however, he could expect the shooting and possibly quite a lot of hitting to begin all over again.

He managed to cross the floor and get himself up onto Sally's shoe before she finished her homework.

Then he had to hang on for a bit while Sally did some travelling of her own, to and from the kitchen, helping to get dinner on the table.

Then he had a *long* climb up Sally's jeans, jumper, collar and hair while dinner was underway. All the time he was expecting doves to appear, angels to drop on top of him and all the rest of it, but they didn't. So maybe Scattletail had been right, and the Other Side had been called off for an urgent discussion with whatever they used instead of brass hammers Up There.

Finally he reached Sally's ear. Still nothing terrible happened to him, as he crept down the first passage to the six-sided chamber. Everything was quiet. Everyone, it seemed, had gone. In the chamber up the stairs, the statue still pointed to the archway with the words LOOK FOR THE RIGHT over it.

'Thank you,' said Muddlespot politely as he passed.

The fountain still played coolly in the courtyard. According to the archway on the far side it was, apparently, still better to GIVE than to RECEIVE.

'Quite,' said Muddlespot, who on his last time through this place had been giving out tar bombs for all he was worth and trying hard not to receive anything that anyone had wanted to give him in exchange. The stairs, wide as a hockey pitch, still led upwards beyond it.

Pitch, pitch, pitch went his footsteps on the stairs; a flat scraping sound echoing with emptiness. *Pitch, pitch, pitch.* Up and up.

Still no one jumped on him.

And here he was. The chamber was exactly the same. The semicircle of statues. The star-studded ceiling. The two great windows, showing the table in the outside world with the Jones family now at dinner. And the central self of Sally, sitting at the same table at the chamber's centre. With one small difference.

She was untying herself.

She had got the loops from around her waist and the gag from off her face. The earmuffs lay discarded on the floor. She was bending down and working on the bonds that held her ankles. That was why she didn't see him when he came in.

'Ahem,' said Muddlespot.

She looked up. She scowled.

And Muddlespot saw why. It wasn't because he had come back. It was because he had *seen her freeing herself*. Tied up tightly at her table, she had remembered what it had felt like in that short moment when the bonds had been off her. And she had thought, after a bit, that maybe she would give it another try, on her own and in private. What she absolutely, definitely didn't want was anyone seeing that she was doing it. Least of all, someone who might think it was because of something *he* had done. She wasn't going to admit that someone might know what she wanted better than she did herself. She didn't like that idea at all.

'What are you doing here?' she snapped.

'Talking to you,' said Muddlespot brightly.

'And who asked you?'

'I thought you might be uncomfortable. But I see you can look after yourself.'

Sally shrugged elaborately. 'They're perfectly comfortable. I just thought I'd do without them for a bit.'

'I see.'

'Don't get any ideas! I'm the good one here. You think you can change that, you've another think coming!'

'I wouldn't dream of it,' said Muddlespot.

And he thought: *I'm the good one here.* Meaning?

'Why do you tie yourself?' he asked innocently.

'It's none of your business.'

'What would you do if you were untied?'

'That's none of your business either.'

'Who would you do it to?'

'Who . . . ?' she said sharply. 'What do you mean?'

'Oh, you know,' said Muddlespot, who didn't.

'Look,' said Sally, folding her arms. 'I do what I do. I am what I am. My choice. Not yours.'

'Oh, quite,' said Muddlespot. 'Your choice. No question. In fact, I wasn't going to talk about you at all. I just wanted to ask . . .'

'*Yes?*'

'. . . about Billie?'

Silence.

'There's nothing to talk about,' said Sally flatly.

'It just seemed a bit clumsy – you know – the way she knocked the table and spilled water over your work like that.'

'It wasn't clumsy at all,' said Sally.

'She doesn't *mean* to be like that,' said Muddlespot. 'Does she?'

Sally said nothing.

'It's hard for her,' Muddlespot went on. 'At school and everything.'

'I know your game,' said Sally. 'I'm not listening.'

'I just wondered' – Muddlespot's gaze had fallen on the foot of the statue of Calm; there seemed to be a tiny crack running up the ankle from the heel – 'in what *way* school was actually so hard?'

'Where are those earmuffs?' asked Sally.

'They were round here somewhere,' said Muddlespot, who had them behind his back.

'I don't need them anyway.'

'Of course not,' said Muddlespot absently. 'You're the good one.' He thought the crack had grown just a fraction. 'Tantrums, tantrums, tantrums,' he mused. '"My pencil sharpener. My calculator. *Your* fault." Is she like that all the time?'

'Yes. I mean, no.'

'No?'

'Not really.'

'I bet when she does something good, they praise her to the skies. Don't they?'

'Shut *up*! And leave me alone!'

'And then they turn round and ask you to—'

'NO!' cried Sally. She had jumped to her feet. Her voice echoed round the chamber. It came from everywhere. It came from outside.

The view through the windows had altered. In the outside world, Sally had jumped to her feet too. She was glaring at her mother across the table. Mum's face stared back in surprise.

'No?' came her voice. 'But Sally . . .'

'It's *her* turn to do the washing-up!'

'But she's still got to do her homework!' pleaded Mum.

'She should have done it yesterday!'

'Why should I have to . . .' murmured Muddle-spot.

'Why should *I* have to do the washing-up just because she can't . . .'

'. . . be bothered . . .' murmured Muddlespot, with a dizzy feeling as if he was pushing at a revolving door that had suddenly started to revolve rather fast.

'. . . be *bothered* to do what she's supposed to do?'

'But you do it so well, sweetheart—'

'Is that right? So maybe I should break things from time to time . . .'

'. . . Like she does,' added Muddlespot.

'Like *SHE* does!' yelled Sally in the chamber of her mind. She flung herself away from the table. It disappeared. A door appeared in the air between two of the statues. She went through it, *SLAM!* and a split second later there was another SLAM! from the outer world, where her body had put her thoughts into action. Stairs appeared beneath her feet and she went up them, *STOMP! STOMP! STOMP! STOMP! STOMP!* echoed by STOMP! STOMP! STOMP! STOMP! from the outer world. Then another door appeared, adorned with tastefully coloured wooden letters which spelled SALLY'S ROOM. That too went *SLAM!* SLAM! On the far side she paused for breath.

In the outside world she was now in her bedroom. She could see it out there, through the windows of her mind. It was neat and tidy, with her clothes put away and nothing on the floor, and her books and alarm clock set square upon her bedside table – all as she had left it this morning.

But inside her mind nothing had changed. She was still in the central chamber with the semicircle of statues around her. And Muddlespot was standing there watching, with a look of innocence on his face.

'I HOPE YOU'RE SATISFIED!' she screamed.

In her bedroom in the outer world there was only silence.

'Don't you feel better now?' said Muddlespot.

'*NO!*'

A bed appeared. She sat down on it and put her face in her hands.

'Nice room,' said Muddlespot, looking out through the windows. 'Very tasteful. Very tidy.'

Sally did not answer.

'Nice picture there,' said Muddlespot. 'You and your sister.'

Sally reached. The picture appeared in her hand.

It *was* a nice picture. It showed two girls; one blonde, one dark. They were the same age as each other, and maybe a couple of years younger than Sally and Billie were now. They were neatly dressed, with their hair washed and brushed and their arms around each other, smiling together at the camera.

'You like each other really, don't you?' whispered Muddlespot.

CRASH!

Muddlespot danced a little jig on the rubble that had once been the statue of Calm.

10: WINDLEBERRY

It's fair to say that reactions in the Jones household varied.

To Mum, run ragged between managing an office during the day and trying to herd her family through the evenings, Sally's outburst was a shock. It was worse because she knew Sally had a point. Billie did drag her heels over her homework, and even when she didn't or said she hadn't got any, there was usually some reason why it just wouldn't be worth the effort of asking her to help wash up. (Most likely because Billie was already in a massive sulk, and standing over her and trying to make her clean each dish properly would just lead to something getting broken, as Sally had said.) So it was just easier to ask Sally. And everything would be done in ten minutes.

Except that now they wouldn't be. Now suddenly, just when she had thought that everything was already as difficult as she could possibly manage, it had got more difficult still. So *her* reaction to Sally's revolt was one of dismay.

Her dismay would increase when she discovered that Sally had chucked the photograph of herself and Billie into the bin. But she hadn't found out about that yet.

Greg, Mum's partner of four years' standing, had spent the whole of supper eating in silence. He always did. He had lasted this long with Mum by taking up the least possible space, both in the house and in conversation. He liked being part of the family and had been pleased to find that he was more or less accepted into it. His desk at work was well decked with family photographs, and his drawers were stuffed with little gifts the girls had given him at odd times. He knew that Billie and Sally were entering their teens and that this was going to mean changes, but he also sensed that to try laying down house rules himself would be like dropping wildcats into a sack and then tying the sack over his head. He preferred to rely, lovingly and trustingly, on

Mum to get them all through it. And also to have his dinner on the table for six o'clock, which would be five minutes after he got in through the door.

His attitude to Sally's performance, when he realized that it had happened, was therefore one of delegated dismay, and it didn't stop him reading the sports pages.

Billie, who was a lot closer to everything that was going on than Greg, was at first as shocked as Mum. She was so surprised that by the time she had caught her breath to have a lovely and *totally* justified yell back at Sally, Sally had slammed the door and was halfway up the stairs. So her next feeling was frustration, followed almost immediately by a feeling of wonderful and secret delight that she would have found very hard to explain, but that lasted all evening and resulted in the best English essay she produced all term.

Shades registered no reaction at all. Except that it was time somebody filled his cat dish.

'I can't cope!' said poor Mum.

'Maybe you should have a word with her,' said Greg, who was so deep into the football transfer market that it took him a little while to think about what his mouth had said automatically. 'When she's calmed down,' he added.

Mum put her head in her hands.

'Should the oven be on?' said Greg helpfully.

'No,' said Mum. 'Sally should have switched it off after she took the cake out.'

Greg tilted his chair back so he could reach the dial without getting up. 'She has. But it's still on. Dodgy connection maybe. There, that's got it.'

'That's dangerous,' said Mum. 'I don't want to wake up and find the house full of smoke.'

Greg stood on his chair to prod the smoke alarm. Nothing happened. 'Battery's gone.'

'Everything's falling to bits,' groaned Mum.

'I'll get it fixed,' said Greg.

(What this meant was that Greg had now said he would get it fixed, and would carry on saying he would get it fixed until Mum either bullied him into it or lost patience and called the electrician herself. And then she would have to miss a morning's work waiting in for the electrician, who would promise to come some time between eight and twelve and would, in fact, arrive at about a quarter to one.)

Mum put her head on the table. 'I want a new job.'

'Mine's taken,' said Greg.

There was dismay, too, in the palaces above the clouds. Voices were raised. Discussions were heated. Fingers jabbed at charts on which lines dipped alarmingly. Angels hurried down corridors clutching sheaves of papers. Juniors followed seniors into meetings, wriggling their brows at bystanders in that way that says, 'Don't ask. It's terribly important, but just don't ask!' And of course that meant the bystanders did ask. And the answer would be an urgent shake of the head and the words, mouthed through the crack of a closing door, 'Sally Jones'.

'It's a disaster!' exclaimed a Seraph, sitting halfway down a table of polished rainwater.

'We've been caught with our cassocks down,' said another. 'We must rectify the situation immediately!'

'I have an attack choir standing by, Archagent.'

On his throne of rose petals the Archagent brooded. His wings were a hundred fathoms in length and rippled with the light of rainbows. They wavered gently, reaching to the distant walls and up into the great dome above him. His eyebrows were small thunderclouds. He had ten thousand of them. When he frowned it was really quite impressive.

He was frowning now.

'The LDC still registers zero, Archagent,' said the last speaker. 'There's time. If we move quickly—'

'Infiltration has occurred,' said the Archagent.

All down the long table, rows of faces watched him. He could look each one of them in the eye. Many times over. And he had also been around for a few thousand years more than any of them. He understood some things they didn't. 'It is a situation of Potential.'

Of course the golden trumpets could blow. The Divine Wind could breathe upon the invader. The ranks of angels could descend with fire upon the mind of Sally Jones, and very quickly there would not be much of this particular infiltrator left.

But once the mind had opened to the ideas of the Enemy, the Enemy could keep coming back. There would be another infiltration, and another, and another. And sometimes it happened that the Enemy chose to meet force with force. Legions of demons and cacodemons might come surging up to meet the powers of Heaven head-on. With consequences that could be *very* undesirable for the subject.

'Ground once lost to the Enemy can never be wholly regained,' he said.

There was a dispirited rustle of feathers down the long table.

'We should cut our losses,' said a young angel. 'Go to Early Martyrdom.'

Another rustle greeted his words. They were thinking about it. If there was a knife fight at school (unheard of at Darlington High, but not impossible). If Sally tried to intervene. If it happened tomorrow, while the LDC still read zero . . .

'Drastic, Simael,' said the Archagent, mentally recording the young angel as someone who, given a red button, would find a reason to press it no matter what. 'Drastic – if direct.'

'Shall I arrange it, sire?'

'No.' He rose from the throne of petals. He was taller than a cathedral spire and as gentle as a cloud in the soft south wind. He looked out of the window of opal down at the little world below. 'This is the Long War,' he said. 'There is disappointment, but no defeat. There is valour, but no victory.'

His thousands of years of struggle had taught him many things. One of them was that however high you got, no one ever told you what was *really* going on.

Another was that, no matter what the LDCs said

at any particular moment, the worst heart on Earth was never very far from Glory, and the purest was never far from Disaster. A soul that had been clean, clean, clean all along was in some ways more vulnerable than one chequered with successes and failures. The Enemy was cunning. He knew how to use self-hatred. He knew how to use shame. For Sally, the smallest failure now could be terrible. It had happened many times before.

'We are not bidden to despair,' he said.

Though indeed, he did feel very close to despair.

'What can we do?' they said to him.

He faced them.

'We shall play the game as it must be played. One to one . . .'

They sighed, reverently.

'. . . And we shall send our best. Send . . .'

He paused. He counted *one, two* . . .

'. . . Agent Windleberry!'

Once more the feathers rustled all down the table. *Windleberry*, the whisper seemed to say. *Our best. Agent Windleberry.*

It is also possible that they said *Windleberry? Oh, the boss's bright-eyed boy! Why's it always Windleberry? Don't know what he sees in him.*

Windleberry? Again! Makes you sick, doesn't it?
Maybe he'll come a cropper this time . . .
That'd be good . . .

If bosses everywhere are the same, then so too are the poor bossed.

One person did share the Archagent's opinion of Windleberry. That was Windleberry himself.

Windleberry was not smug or self-satisfied or conceited. He was just the best. He knew it.

No one carried angelic perfection to the same lengths that he did. No one watched more sleeplessly, praised more mightily or fought the good fight more fiercely. His jaw was long and lean and square. His forehead was high and square. Under his crisp white shirt his pectorals were massive – and square. His wings were made of bright white light (and they were square too). His flaming eyes were shaded behind Ray-Bans of translucent ebony. His bow tie was vermillion and his tuxedo was a daring cream. His long, square fingers flew lightly over the keys of his tenor sax, and the notes he played made angels weep – for the right reasons.

He had served in every heavenly department and was thorough in everything he did. Other angels marked the sparrow's fall, but Windleberry gave it marks out of ten and made it fall again if it scored less than three. Other angels counted the hairs on a human's head, but Windleberry clipped a tiny numbered label to each one and offered them around for sponsorship. He had spent a century on the watchtowers. He had given artists and poets such visions of inspiration that most of them had been locked up before their work could be completed. He had reduced the composer Handel to tears over writing the Hallelujah chorus. He had slain dragons, carried stars and sung so loudly in the countertenor line that the angelic choirmasters had despaired of ever getting the balance right.

He had served with the cupids. Cupids have a culture all of their own. It comes from doing what they do stark naked and showing their bums all the time. You go with the cupids with a name like 'Windleberry' – you *have* to be tough.

He never carped, he never questioned, he never came back to complain about how difficult it was. That was why his bosses liked him. They just pointed him and he went. And then there would be no more problem. The only thing with Windleberry was that you had to remember to shout 'stop'.

All the heavenly hosts turned out for him on the day

he went to be guardian to Sally Jones. They lined the crystal corridors and they thronged the battlements. He stalked past them with his jaw jutting, his fingers curled around the grip of his sax case and his heels going *clip-clip-clip* on the paving that was made of the rose of dawn. He looked neither right nor left. He said no goodbyes.

Behind him trailed the briefing choir, singing his instructions in dutiful plainsong:

> *'O-o-oh A-Agent Windleb'ry, champion of li-ight,*
> *Yo-oung Sa-ally Jo-ones is lost to the ni-ight.*
> *Our bri-ightest ho-ope in Darlington Row*
> *Has be-en infiltra-ated by-y the Foe.*
> *Your mi-ission, if to accept it you cho-ose:*
> *Apply to the butt of the fiend some well-planted*
>   *sho-oes.*
> *Oh spe-ed you no-ow for glo-ory beckons,*
> *This choir will self destru-uct in fi-i-ive seconds.*
> *A-a-a-men.'*

They accompanied him to the very top of a high watchtower. And there, true to their word, they vanished into little puffs of purple smoke.

Agent Windleberry paused on the brink. All along

the battlements, the eyes of the Host were on him. Below his feet was the great gulf: the darkness, the nebulae, the stars, the Earth. He looked down upon it, at the tiny, tiny gem of the world.

No angel could be unmoved by that sight. So forlorn. So deadly, like a beautiful, poisoned flower.

Because it *was* deadly. The only way an angel could get there was to fall. Falling is easy. An angel that falls can fall a very long way. It's the Not Falling Any Further that's hard. It was said that Pandemonium itself was founded by a group of angels that, so to speak, had simply got off at the wrong floor.

But that was a long time ago.

Windleberry saw the sunlight playing across half the Earth. He saw the border of night and day, a ring of twilight forever moving, forever in the same place. He saw the galaxy of human souls shining in the darkness of their lives.

He put one foot out over the void.

And he fell.

11: ISMAEL

Certain very-well-trained soldiers on Earth, when they have to land secretly in enemy territory, do what they call a 'HALO' jump. That's 'HALO' as in High Altitude Low Opening. You jump out of a plane that's flying very high up, where it can't be shot down. You then fall and fall and fall and fall, and at the very last moment, when you are least likely to be spotted or picked up on someone's radar, you open your parachute. And you land safely.

That's the idea.

Angels, when they are landing in dangerous territory, do what they call the 'NO HALO' jump. That is, before you jump you switch your halo off.

It also helps if you are not accompanied by bright

lights, the appearance of new stars, tongues of fire or claps of thunder. All these things tend to give your position away.

Windleberry, of course, executed his jump perfectly. He always did. And he made his landing not on the top of Sally's head but somewhere else. He had some reconnaissance to do.

The mind he came to was not like Sally's mind. The corridors were narrow. They were also ill-lit, because the person they belonged to was on the edge of sleep. In this mind, if you didn't have a very clear idea of where you were going, you ended up in the same place three times out of five. There was one huge room near the bottom where most of the ideas were kept. They wandered about in the half-darkness, getting in each other's way and occasionally eating one another. Around it, other rooms were arranged in no kind of order, stacking up on top of each other like badly built apartment blocks.

Windleberry trudged up endless flights of stairs. The stairs looked as if they saw more use from a skateboard than a pair of shoes. In the gloom, little things scuttled and squeaked around his feet. Somewhere a voice shrieked 'Sally!' in rage tinged with tears.

In a dark passage high up in the mind, he found the door he was looking for. It had a sign on it. The sign read:

ISMAEL
GUARDIAN ANGEL

He knocked. There was a sudden movement inside.

'Who's there?' called a voice.

'Agent Windleberry,' he said. And then – since he realized, with some broad-mindedness, that Ismael had been out here for some years and might not even know the name 'Windleberry' or associate it with the long string of glories and achievements that were sung in the corridors above the clouds – he added, 'I'm assigned to Sally.'

More sounds followed, as if things were quickly being swept off a desk or table.

'Come in,' said the voice.

Windleberry entered. It was a small, gloomy office, lit by a single anglepoise lamp that was perched on one of a number of piles of paperwork that half covered the desk in the middle of the room. The walls were lined with cabinets, shelves and one large cupboard. There were two empty chairs on the door side of the desk. A strange smell hung in the air. On the far side of the desk sat the guardian angel.

Well, yes, it *was* an angel – just. It looked like an angel that had been dragged through sixteen thorn hedges backwards and dropped a couple of times off a high cliff. It looked as if it had at some point been on the wrong end of a barrage of tar bombs, and had never quite got the stains out. It wore the regulation dark glasses, tuxedo and bow tie, but the tie was undone and the tuxedo wasn't so much rumpled as in deep trauma.

'Well, goodness me,' said the angel through gritted teeth. 'What a surprise.'

Windleberry sniffed the air. Strange . . .

'To what do I owe the pleasure?' said the angel.

'Top Priority,' said Windleberry. 'Sally's been infiltrated.'

'Shame,' said Ismael, tipping back his chair.

'Intelligence suggests that it was witnessing

continuous non-compliant behaviour from Billie that made Sally vulnerable.'

'Intelligence is welcome to come down and see if they can do better with Billie than I can.'

'It's no laughing matter,' said Windleberry. 'Sally is key.'

'Why?'

Behind his translucent ebony Ray-Bans, Windleberry frowned. *Why* wasn't a question that got asked a lot above the clouds. One of the reasons it didn't get asked much was that the answers were never very satisfactory. They tended to involve long lectures about stretching measuring lines across the Earth and entering the storehouses of the snow, and other things which, to any thinking observer, were rather beside the point.

'Because she's good,' he ventured.

'Why?'

'Because she is. Or would be, if she wasn't being interfered with.'

'*She's* being interfered with? I guess you've not read any of my reports. No surprise. I don't expect anyone up there actually reads what I—'

'Yes, I have.'

Windleberry had prepared for his mission with

his usual diligence. He had read the reports on Sally, on Billie, on Sally's mum, on Greg and on Sally's dad. He had read the reports on Charlie B, on Ameena, on Janey, on Cassie, on David, on Chris and on all the other students in Sally's class. He had read the reports on their teachers. He had read *Paradise Lost*. He had read the reports on Mr Granger and Mrs Kemp and the driver of the number 86 bus. He had filed a complaint that there was no report on Shades the cat, which had got him some funny looks up in the Records Department.

But yes, he had read the reports on Billie. There was quite a file on Billie.

'Billie's a good kid,' said Ismael fiercely. 'That's what you guys don't get. You say, "Why can't she be like Sally?" She can't be like Sally *because* of Sally. Sally's always there, always better than her at everything. Better marked. Better liked. Just better. All the time. How do you *think* she's going to take that?'

'There's no excusing—'

'No? OK. So Sally gets to be better at everything. But why is it *Sally* who gets to have 20:20 vision, and Billie who has to wear glasses? Why is it that *Sally* can eat what she likes and Billie comes out in spots? That's just not fair!'

'It doesn't have to be fair. You know that.'

'Yay, *verily*! So I tell Billie it's better she comes second to Sally in everything and all she has to do is not mind about it. How far's that going to get me? You know what? When I saw Sally throw that fit of hers this evening, and all that posse she had looking after her flapped off to have their wrists slapped, you know what I did? I *cheered*. I abso-lutely *rocked* it in here. Just for a moment I wasn't playing uphill. No hard feelings, Winifred, but my bedtime prayer tonight is that you won't get too far too quickly.'

'You misunderstand the mission,' said Windleberry coldly. 'It is not a choice between one and the other. There can be no compromise. No meeting place—'

He broke off. He sniffed the air again. 'You *smoke*?'

'Officially, it's frankincense,' said Ismael, tipping his chair. '*Un*officially, I smoke, swig, snort and chew anything I can get my hands on just to keep my nerves steady and my eyes on what she's doing. Don't give me a lecture, freshie. Wait till you've been down here a while and we'll see how you do. Right now you stink of soap, yay verily.'

Windleberry leaned across the desk. 'Maybe you're right,' he breathed. 'Maybe they don't read your

123

reports upstairs. But they read mine. I'll be filing one about this meeting, as it happens. What would it *not* be good for me to write?'

Ismael untipped his chair. He too leaned forward. 'Ugly talk, Winifred.'

'It's "Windleberry". But you don't need to remember that. Because it won't be me you'll be answering to if you don't bring Billie round. You know that posse of Sally's that flapped off? They didn't just get their wrists slapped. They were sent up to be . . . Forgiven.'

There was a short, thick silence. Angels are perfect in every way. So the very worst thing you can do to one is to find something to forgive it for.

'Sure,' said Ismael at last. 'I'll work on Billie.'

'Better get started, then,' said Windleberry coldly.

'Billie will get home,' said Ismael. 'But not for your sake, Wimple. *Or* Sally's. She'll get there because in the end she'll want to.'

'You need to be right about that.'

'It's no business of yours if I am or I'm not. And I kinda hope you're about to get out of here. You're making my feng shui come out in spots.'

Windleberry looked at Ismael. His mouth was a short straight line.

Ismael looked back. So was his.

Windleberry put a hand to his Ray-Bans of translucent ebony.

There's a reason why angels wear dark glasses most of the time. It is because of the light in their eyes, which is the pure fire of Heaven. For an angel to touch his glasses is like a gunslinger stroking the butt of his Colt .45 in a crowded saloon.

Ismael put his hand to his glasses too. As if to say – yeah, he could probably manage a couple of sparks himself.

Windleberry straightened. He strode majestically from the room. His measured steps went *clop, clop, clop*, fading down the passages of Billie's mind. Ismael stayed motionless, watching the door.

After a moment the cupboard coughed. A small gout of yellow smoke exuded from the keyhole. A voice said, 'Izzie gone?'

'Yeah. You can come out now.'

The cupboard door opened. Out sidled Scattletail, shiftily, like a word dropping from his own mouth. The smell of smoke was suddenly stronger, and it had a sulphurous flavour.

'Thought he'd sniffed you out there,' said Ismael.

There were more thumps from the cupboard. Out came the inner self of Billie. She was wearing

125

her pyjamas, which these days were more brown than pink and too small for her. She was not, of course, where she should have been at this time, which was in bed.

'What a stiff!' grumbled Scattletail. '"You misunderstand the mission." Would yer b'lieve it! Where did you get him from?'

'I was like that once – I think.'

'Want me to wise him up?'

'Let him find out for himself. Where were we?'

'It was my deal,' said Billie.

The chairs were drawn up. A much-handled pack of cards appeared from a desk drawer. *Flick, flick, flick* they went across the paper-scattered desk.

A little while later, Scattletail said 'Three jacks.'

'Dang!' said Ismael.

'So Billie skips the washing-up again.'

'Suits me,' said Billie.

'Not yet she doesn't. Deal.'

Flick, flick, flick went the cards.

A little while later, Ismael said 'Dang!' again.

'You need to smarten up your play, buddy.'

'At least I've got you where I can see you,' growled Ismael. 'Deal.'

*

The path of Truth is narrow. It twists in the darkness. It is watched, by eyes that are not kind. It is easy to stray.

Windleberry crossed the landing of the Jones household like a nightwalker threading his way through bad streets. He went quickly, warily, looking all around him. He did not try to hide. Hiding only meant that the danger came to you.

The night crawled with noises. Voices called, angrily, drunkenly, from outside. Car tyres swished on wet road. Headlights turned in the windows, sending irregular, square-edged beams like searchlights across the ceiling. In the shadows was a deeper shadow with wide eyes and pointed ears. It was the shape of Shades the cat.

Windleberry walked on. He did not falter. He knew the Enemy was near.

The Enemy! He lay in the clothes-strewn jungle of Billie's room behind him. He waited in the unknown reaches of Sally's room ahead. He rose humming in the sounds of late-night football that drifted up the stairs from the sitting room, where Greg lay dozing on the sofa and young men slashed each other with studs upon the screen. He watched, from the darkness, as the tiny figure of the angel passed.

Shades watched too. When Windleberry looked back, he saw that the cat's head had turned to follow him. Cats see things that others do not.

He passed through the crack beneath Sally's door. Sally's clothes were folded and put away. She was reading in bed. The book in her hands was *Paradise Lost*. Her bedside light was an anglepoise, directed low over her page. It threw huge shadows over the walls. The black shape of the book. The black shape of Sally. The shadow of the bed posts, the lamp stand, the cupboards and desk and chest of drawers. Sally's face was bright light and shadow. Cheeks and lips glowed. One eye glinted. The other was in darkness.

In the slanting light some of the shadows had horns.

Windleberry stepped forward.

12: FIRST MEETING

The lights were still on in Sally's mind. They had a subdued yellow glow, like a hotel foyer late at night when the staff are still sitting up for the last few guests who are lost in the fleshpots of town.

There was even a desk in the first six-sided chamber. With a sign on it, marked RECEPTION. There was a young person sitting behind the desk. Windleberry thought he recognized her.

'Excuse me, miss,' he said.

She gave him a cool smile and a glance over a pair of glasses that – when he looked at them – were obviously not worn to improve her 20:20 eyesight. 'Yes?'

'You're Sally, aren't you?'

She leaned forward and tapped the desk sign:

RECEPTION. And then she resumed her pose and her smile. 'Yes?'

'Uh – checking in, please.'

'Have you got a reservation?'

'You'll have a room for me somewhere,' he said firmly.

(There always is a room somewhere, in every mind. The booking is made before the mind is born.)

'In what name, please?'

Windleberry drew himself up. 'The Name Above All Names, miss.'

'Cool.' She made a note.

He waited. After a moment he asked, 'Do I get a key?'

'We keep the keys.'

'I see.' He waited some more.

She looked up. 'Yes?'

'Where do I find the – uh – manager?'

She gestured vaguely with her pen. 'Upstairs somewhere.'

'I'll see you there.'

She did not answer so he left her. When he looked back, both she and the desk had gone.

He passed under a high crystal archway. He climbed a flight of broad stairs. Here was another chamber, much like the first, with six sides and an archway in each one. Down long, softly lit galleries, through walls and floors and ceilings of gently tinted crystal, Windleberry saw innumerable successions of archways and pillars and chambers, vastly intricate. Music seemed to be playing somewhere. He listened to it.

After a moment he decided he didn't like it. Whoever was playing was overworking the rhythm section.

In the middle of the chamber rose a half-statue of a man with a full beard, crowned with leaves, arm outstretched, carved out of ice. Over one archway were the words LOOK FOR THE RIGHT. The outstretched arm of the statue pointed to the archway just to the left of that one.

'Hmmm,' said Windleberry.

But he went the way that he was pointed. It turned a corner, turned corners some more, and then seemed to double back on itself as if it were teasing him. But eventually he came to a court where a fountain was playing. The fountain seemed to be spouting purple ink.

Windleberry crossed the open space. On the far side was the higher, wider arch with the words IT IS BETTER TO GIVE THAN TO RECEIVE.

Someone had splashed paint over them. And had daubed the word BREAKOUT! all over them in green.

'I see,' muttered Windleberry.

In their niches, the statues brooded silently. Their blank eyes looked down on him. *You wouldn't happen to have a scrubbing brush, would you?* they seemed to say. *And – er – some soap?*

There was another flight of stairs, wide and very long. Windleberry climbed steadily up it. At the top was another arch. Beyond it was another chamber. This was the place.

The ceiling was set with stars. A pantheon of crystal statues stood in a semicircle around the centre of the room. Opposite, curving round the far wall, were two huge arched windows. They showed only darkness, because Sally had just switched her light out.

Windleberry looked slowly around the room. Something was wrong . . .

One of the statues was wearing a beret. It wasn't that.

Another had star-shaped sunglasses. It wasn't that either.

The statue of Truth was now called TRUFE. She also carried a guitar.

'There's something at work here,' muttered Windleberry.

On the base of the statue of Wisdom were the words WIZDUM ROOLZ OK.

'Sinister . . .' breathed Windleberry. And close, he thought. He could smell it. But it wasn't the statues.

It was the door.

There it was; a small, low doorway, in that place where all the archways were high and drew the eye upwards. It was in an area of the wall that was heavily tinted, and was itself tinted so that it was fully opaque. From where he stood, Windleberry could see a long way down many corridors of Sally's crystal mind. He could see out into the world. But he couldn't see beyond the little door.

He went still, like a deer that scents a tiger. He listened.

Nothing.

He drew a long breath and . . .

Yes.

'It shouldn't be *this close*,' he muttered.

Not this close to the centre of her mind.

Softly he stole to the door. It was open, just a crack. Noiselessly, he went in.

It was a small chamber, with opaque walls. There was nothing in it. No clutter, no shut-away nightmares, no madness chained and gibbering to the wall. There was just the trap door.

There were no signs on the trap door. Neither KEEP OUT nor WELCOME. There was no lock on it either. He lifted the trap and looked down.

Intelligence had talked confidently of fifty fathoms of diamond block. Intelligence was out of date, it seemed. Things had changed in Sally's mind. The diamond was gone. There were no steps going down. No lift, no ladder, not even a rope. There was only darkness.

The darkness that led down to Pandemonium.

He felt it calling to him, whispering from below. *You just step over the void and drop*, it said. *Drop. You won't be the first, Windleberry. You won't be the last either. Drop. Now.*

Softly, he closed it again. From his pack he took a short length of the bright wire of Swiftness. He curled it lovingly in his hands, and snapped it into three pieces. He took out two batteries, charged with Virtue. He took out a small sheet of the silver of Prudence. He took out a primer of Decision, placing it carefully down on the floor so that it would not trigger. And then, very gently and carefully, he took out two transparent tubes filled with a liquid the colour of amber. He held his breath.

Truth comes in many forms and may be used in many ways. But Pure Truth, pure one hundred per cent distilled Truth, is very rare. And it is very, very explosive.

With rock-steady hands, Windleberry clipped one tube to either side of the primer. He used the short, bright lengths of Swiftness to link the primer to the batteries and the sheet of silver, and teased the sheet and the wire into position so that if anyone tried to lift the trap door from below the sheet would make contact with the wire and the circuit would be complete.

You couldn't block the trap door. Not for ever. Windleberry knew that. You *could* stand over it with a fiery sword and guard it for an eternity, but in Windleberry's experience that wasn't very productive either. On the other hand, a couple of tubes of Truth would give anyone coming up from below something to think about. Assuming, that is, that they left that person any head to think with.

Windleberry tiptoed back into the main chamber. Gently he pushed the door not quite closed – just as it had been when he'd first seen it. He looked at it for a moment. But there was nothing to give his little device away. He let out his breath. He looked around the chamber, at the statues in their hippy guises. He studied the deliberate misspellings. He smiled, tolerantly.

He happened to be looking in exactly the wrong

direction when Muddlespot waddled smugly round from behind the statue of Trufe.

Muddlespot was looking the wrong way too.

So neither of them saw each other.

For about one-sixth of a second.

'AAAAHGHGHA-AGHGHAGH!'

'AAAAHGHGHA-AGHGHAGH!'

screamed the angel, jaw dropping to about the level of his knee. Then, as instinct took over and his hands flew to break out the tenor sax, stand and an assortment of sheet music specially written to cause maximum damage at close range, 'YOU PUNK! I'M GONNA FRY YA! I'LL BLAST YA ALL THE WAY OUT TO JUPITER! EAT DEATH, SCUM! DIE, DIE, DIE!!!'

screamed Muddlespot, eyes popping out to the length of his nose. Then, as instinct took over and his claws fumbled frantically in his sack for his trident (guaranteed to pierce the heavenliest of armour at close range), 'YOU STIFF! I'M GONNA FORK YA INSIDE OUT AND PLAY NOODLES WITH YER ENTRAILS! EAT DEATH, YER PIG! DIE, DIE, DIE!!!'

136

'Hold it,' said Sally.

She had appeared between them. Like lightning, she stuffed a handful of socks down the mouth of the tenor sax and plonked two more pairs of rolled-up socks on the tines of Muddlespot's trident. And she caught both of them in an armlock. 'Let's get one thing straight, you guys,' she said. 'If you're staying, you don't fight. And no shouting either.'

Windleberry winced. For a top-flight celestial agent to be given a Chinese burn by a fourteen-year-old was a new experience. Not to say painful and humiliating. But that was how it was when you were an idea in someone's head. They could do anything they liked to you. They could twist you, shut you up, or take you apart to see what you were made of. The one thing they couldn't do was stop you coming back.

Ouch. He hoped the watchtowers were not watching too closely. The tips of Muddlespot's trident wavered before his eyes. The one un-socked spike still looked very sharp.

'Uh . . . Do you mind . . . ?' he gasped.

'Oh. Sorry.' Sally jammed another pair of socks onto the trident.

'Where did the socks come from?' said Muddle-spot dazedly. He was rubbing his elbow where Sally had released him.

'I know where my socks are,' said Sally flatly. '*And* I keep them in pairs. All of them. Not that I wear them much any more. I'll take these. No weapons. And *I* choose the music here, mister.' She frisked them both, removing the sax, the trident, Windleberry's shoulder-holstered harmonica and a couple of tar bombs that Muddlespot hadn't even known he still had.

'Now, I'm off to bed . . .' she said, carting it all off in an armful.

'Oh, and one more thing,' she added. 'No one gets to whisper to me after the lights go out. I want to sleep with a clear conscience.'

'Glad to hear it,' said Windleberry, also rubbing his elbow and glowering at his rival.

'I said clear, not clean, mister.'

'So what do we do until morning?' said Muddle-spot.

'Take a break,' said Sally over her shoulder. 'Like someone said, there'll be a room for you somewhere. There may even be a bed.'

Muddlespot looked at Windleberry. Windleberry looked at Muddlespot.

'You can decide between you who gets it,' said Sally.

13: DARLINGTON HIGH

Darlington High is a school like any other school. It's a battleground.

It's the sort of battleground where there are lots of battles all going on at once. And most of the people in them haven't a clue who's winning. But they're beginning to think it isn't them.

There's the usual battle to keep cigarettes, alcohol and drugs out of the school. It's fought by nearly everyone, mostly by saying loudly that there definitely isn't a problem whenever they're asked if there is.

There's also the battle to suppress the muffin racket, which is run by certain enterprising Year Sevens whose bus happens to stop outside the bakery. This one is fought mainly by the staff, by means of confiscations, detentions, letters to parents, lectures in assemblies, etcetera. The pupils of Darlington High listen dutifully and take care to conceal their crumbs. The staff are on their own with this one.

There's the long-running guerrilla war over dress code, which took a sharp turn for the worse about a year ago when the governors decided that it would look so much *smarter* and instil a much stronger *ethos* if they replaced the old sweater with a V neck, collared shirt and tie. Introducing ties to a thousand twelve- to eighteen-year-olds of course results in nine hundred and ninety-nine examples of tie abuse to make a governor shudder. Sally J, Form 9c, the exception.

There's the battle fought by all lonely teachers everywhere to convince their class of thirty-odd students that *this* subject and *this* lesson – a double Chemistry period on atomic structure, say – is worthy not only of study but of *love*, and will be the *key* to their future lives if only they could open their eyes to see. It is fought and lost in parallel with the losing of thirty-odd battles to stay awake during the same time. (Last term, an inventive Biology teacher actually won all thirty-one battles simultaneously during a lesson on sexual reproduction, with some creative teaching techniques that afterwards involved much correspondence between the Headmistress and parents. In the end it went down as a Pyrrhic victory, and the teacher is now in another profession.)

And there's the fight that everyone fights, within themselves, every moment of every day. The opening skirmishes begin with the bleep of the alarm and continue through the dazed, one-word conversations that take place over breakfast. The rumble of the traffic and the hoot of horns are the first bombardments, and by the time everyone slouches into their school or office, shaking off the rainwater and stretching their eyes, battle is truly joined.

Battle was joined in the mind of Mrs Goodwin that morning, as 9c arrived for their serving of double Maths.

'*The dear young things,*' bellowed her guardian angel into her left ear. '*I've so much to offer them . . . What I say now may stay with them for the rest of their lives . . .* ' The angel was hanging by a thread finer than gossamer, shouting through a megaphone to get his thoughts across. Little beads of sweat were forming on his forehead. He was acutely aware that his opposite number was suspended by Mrs Goodwin's other ear, shouting things such as '*The ungrateful toads . . . Look at them. The best years of my life I've given to them, and what . . .*' (Neither angel nor fiend actually dared to enter Mrs Goodwin's mind at that moment, just in case they got made to sit down and do double Maths.)

What the angel didn't know was that the fiends were working in pairs that morning. And while one was doing the bellowing-into-the-ear, a second was undercover, busily sawing at the angel's thread.

The thread parted. The angel fell.

So did Mrs Goodwin.

'That's *enough*!' she screeched. 'If you can't come in quietly, you'll all be staying in at break!'

In the inner chamber of Sally's mind, the Inner Sally put her head in her hands. 'Great,' she said. 'We haven't even started and already she's getting stressy.'

She was in her uniform, neat, tie straight, shirt tucked in, sitting at a table exactly like the ones in the classroom. Behind her stood Muddlespot and Windleberry, watching each other out of the corners of their eyes. They weren't fighting. They weren't even yelling at each other. They were just standing there with their arms tightly folded, watching each other's every move.

Every – tiny – move.

Just let him turn his back for a moment, they were both thinking. *Only for a moment. Please . . .*

143

You might say an uneasy truce reigned.

'I need a muffin,' said Sally.

'Remember,' Mrs Goodwin was saying. 'When multiplying fractions, what do we do . . . ?'

Windleberry waited.

Muddlespot waited.

Windleberry waited.

'. . . The lowest common denominator,' said Mrs Goodwin. 'To find this you need to multiply both sides . . .'

'One Sally over Zero Muffins equals Infinity times Bad Day,' groaned Sally.

It was Muddlespot who blinked first.

'Flick some Blu-Tack at her?' he ventured.

'Be serious, will you?' said Sally.

'All right,' said Muddlespot, feeling hurt. 'All right. Please yourself.'

'I could get the hiccups,' said Sally.

'Hiccups?'

'Very serious, hiccups. Hysteria. Sickbay. Could take half a morning. I've seen it done.'

'Oooh yes! Yes – hiccups. That's it! Brilliant!'

'Just kidding.'

'Oh.'

After a moment, Muddlespot tried again. 'It's *such* a nice day out there . . .'

'It's raining,' said Sally flatly.

'Well, it would be a nice day if . . .'

'I'm not looking.'

Interesting, thought Windleberry.

Mrs Goodwin handed a question paper round the class. Sally opened her book and began to write.

She's still attentive, hardworking, thought Windleberry. *No change there.*

'The kid beside you's signalling,' whispered Muddlespot.

'That's Charlie B,' sighed Sally. 'He'll be stuck on question two.'

She still wants to help her friends.

Rain spattered on the window.

'What's three-eights times four-fifths?' asked Sally.

'Fifteen over thirty-two,' said Windleberry promptly.

'Actually, it's three-tenths. When I want your help, mister, I'll ask for it.'

Maybe all I need to do is keep my mouth shut, thought Windleberry.

'Why don't you pass him the wrong answer?' whispered Muddlespot. 'That'd teach him to interrupt you.'

'Because he trusts me. It wouldn't be fair.'

Interesting, thought Windleberry.

But still dangerous.

It was never dull in the mind of Billie Jones.

It could be frustrating, infuriating, maddening and soul-destroying, especially for anyone charged with keeping Billie on the straight and narrow. Expecting Billie to stay on the straight and narrow was like showing a kitten a bucket of cold water and expecting it to wash itself. With soap.

But it was *never* dull.

During Madame Guisel's French lesson, a crowd wearing liberty caps burst into the central chamber, seized the idea of Madame Guisel and carried her off screaming to the guillotine.

Most of the lesson on Tudors and Stuarts was devoted to the trial for High Treason of Mrs Clough (Head of History) and her subsequent sentencing to Death by Marriage to Henry VIII, presiding judge Lady Billie Jones, clerk of the court Thomas Cromwell (or possibly Oliver Cromwell – Billie didn't really care what he called himself so long as he was on *her* side).

During Art, an idea that looked very like Sally got up from where she sat, gave the idea of Charlie B a passionate kiss and died of a heart attack brought on by the instant hardening of her arteries.

Ismael ignored it all. He kept his eyes on Scattletail, and the way he dealt the cards.

In Geography the class was studying Arizona. Up at the front, Mr Bellows talked about rainfall. There wasn't much in Arizona, it seemed.

There was plenty outside.

Scattletail sucked his cheeks. 'I'll see your D minus,' he said, 'an' raise you a yawn and a look out of the winder.'

Geography ground to a finish. The rain lifted. It stayed off, malevolently, long enough for Mrs Bedding to decide that she could hold 9c's hockey class on the sports pitch. Then it came on again just lightly enough to make everyone miserable without forcing Mrs Bedding to admit that she had been wrong.

In the chamber of Sally's mind it was raining too. She stood there in her hockey gear with her knees going grey in the cold.

'I don't suppose either of you guys know how to

play?' she growled through chattering teeth.

'Know how to . . . ?' exclaimed Windleberry. 'I made the Crystal Sea 'B' team last year!'

'Oooh, aren't you special!' simpered Muddlespot, who was tired of getting nowhere with Sally.

'And what would you know about it?'

'Me?' Muddlespot shrugged. 'I never liked sports.'

'You surprise me. Sally – you need to mark their winger.'

'That's what I'm doing, aren't I?'

'Call this marking? You need to be closer. And watch the space behind, because that's where they'll— *Arggh!* There she goes! *After her!*'

'But I'll get hurt!'

'Never mind that – run!'

'But I'll get *hurt!*'

'Not if you *go* for it! Go for the ball! There – good! . . . *HEY!*'

The floor shook and the chamber turned on its side. All three of them went flying. In the outer world, Sally landed flat on her face in the mud. 'Ow!' she said.

'Ow!' said the Inner Sally, from underneath Muddlespot.

Windleberry leaped to his feet, eyes blazing through his Ray-Bans. 'Foul!' he cried. 'Foul! Get after her! Hack her shins! Stamp on her—'

'Oooh, yes,' said Muddlespot. 'Do hack her!'

'Hack her,' said Windleberry, giving him a filthy look. 'But in the *right spirit*!'

'Forget it,' groaned Sally, picking herself up to the sounds of distant cheering from the team that had just scored. 'I don't have to be good at everything . . .'

And then there was Mrs Bunnidy.

There is a special place in Heaven for Mrs Bunnidy. It probably has a lock and key.

She is one of those dear souls who, while never in danger of ending up on the racks of Pandemonium herself, manages to help quite a number of people that way in the course of her lifetime.

She is an *excellent* preschool and early primary age teacher. Children from the ages of three and a half to six adore her, and she adores them, although she does not let them know it. She talks to them as they need to be talked to, encourages them as they need to be encouraged, and over a year with her they will flower and grow beautifully. Secretly, Mrs Bunnidy would like to be six herself. She knows how it's done.

Mrs Bunnidy does not understand that people don't stay six for ever.

Give her a class of juniors to supervise, and she'll put her hands on her hips and say in that bright sing-song voice of hers, ♪'Now – when you're *all*♭ sitting nice-ly . . .'♩ She won't see the looks on their faces. She can't.

Ask her to take a Year Nine assembly and she'll expect to escort them from the class to the hall herself. Possibly holding hands.

Mutinous fidgeting gets put down to naughtiness. Stares of disbelief do not register. And never, ever think of trying to talk to Mrs Bunnidy about it. You might hurt her feelings. Or worse.

You might end up on the Naughty Step.

Of course, she's not a regular teacher at secondary school. But secondary schools get short of staff, and when they are they look around and take whoever's available. And when they get someone like Mrs Bunnidy, they put them in charge of something they think can't do any harm.

Like, er, Food Tech.

Big mistake.

*

'Pair up, children,' said Mrs Bunnidy. 'Two to an oven.'

'Children?' said Muddlespot indignantly. 'She called us *children*?'

'She's like that,' said the Inner Sally, putting out flour, eggs, sugar and butter on the kitchen surface that had appeared in the middle of the chamber. 'Just ignore it. The main thing is not to touch the cupboard with the door that keeps falling off its hinges.'

(Darlington High's Food Tech block was the pride of the school when it opened on the site of the old staff car park. That was five years ago, and nowadays bits of it rattle and shake more than they should. The Food Tech Department keep asking the Headmistress to talk to the Governors about funding some renewals. The Head says she will, she really will, as soon as they have cleared one or two very high priority items that are already in the system. Like finding somewhere for her to park her car.)

'Richard, will you share with David, please?' said Mrs Bunnidy.

'Oh boy,' muttered the Inner Sally. 'Food fight of the century, here we go.'

'And I want to see you all cooking *nicely* . . .'

'I give it five minutes,' said Sally, mixing her flour and baking powder.

Through the windows of her mind they saw Charlie B draw a floury hand across his mouth, giving himself a white moustache and goatee beard. Someone out there shrieked with laughter.

'Billie, haven't you got a partner?'

'Late as usual,' grumbled Sally in the privacy of her mind. 'You think she'd learn.'

'We'll find someone for you . . .'

Sally stiffened mid-knead. 'Oh no,' she said. 'No, please no . . .'

'Has anyone not got a partner?' Mrs Bunnidy's voice was getting ominously nearer.

'Time to look busy,' said Sally. She bowed her head over the idea of her bowl and focused fiercely on the thoughts of teaspoon and bicarbonate of soda.

'Sally . . .'

'*I am invisible*,' whispered Sally. '*I am not here. I am not* . . .'

(It was at this point that, out there in the Food Tech room, the first fistful of flour flew through the air behind Mrs Bunnidy's back.)

'Sally, wouldn't you like to share with Billie?'

Slowly, like a space marine who hears the slither of alien goo behind her, Sally turned. The mutinous face of Billie swam in her vision. Billie was clutching a crumpled bag of flour as if it was a grenade.

'There you are, Billie. Cook nicely together.' ♬

Only Mrs Bunnidy could have thought this was a good idea.

14: THE BATTLE OF FOOD TECH BLOCK

There are times when Heaven trembles.

It's not when wars are declared, harvests fail or dictators seize power. These things are expected and so far as Heaven is concerned they don't change very much.

It's the little things that matter.

It's when someone might laugh or cry, and doesn't know which until the moment they do it. It's when they might say a kind word, but forget to do so. It's when they might cross the road and meet someone, or they might not.

It's at times like these that the angels hold their breath.

And when two sisters face one another by an oven door – that's when they shriek '*ALERT!*' in High C.

'What are you making?' said Billie suspiciously.

'Muffins,' said Sally.

'It's supposed to be scones.'

'I asked her and she said I could. I missed getting my muffin because Mrs Goodwin held us back at break.' (Sally really hadn't meant to sound as though it was Billie's fault that the class had been held back. But of course Billie had been one of the ones Mrs Goodwin had snapped at, and so of course that's how it sounded to Billie. That's the way the muffin crumbles.)

Billie looked at Sally's preparations, which were already well advanced. 'I'll make muffins too,' she said. (And of course that was meant to annoy Sally. And of course it shouldn't have done. But it did.)

Billie plonked down her bag of flour and rummaged in the drawer for a whisk. Her fingers closed upon it. And the Billie in the Food Tech Block put that on the surface too.

But the Billie in the inner chamber of her own mind took that whisk and brandished it like a battle-axe in the face of her twin. 'Come on, you twerp!' she yelled. 'You just *try* to tell me how! *You just try!*'

'Hey,' said Ismael.

155

'She's *such* a know-all!' cursed Billie. 'She will, I bet you!'

Ismael looked across the little table. On the far side, the eyes of Scattletail peeped over the tops of his cards. They were deep and dark. They did not blink.

'Remember,' chimed the maddening voice of Mrs Bunnidy. 'Your dough should be *light*. Think of *air*, children, as you knead it. Think of butterflies and air.'

Ismael looked at his own hand. Why was he never the dealer at times like this?

Scattletail's eyes were like a wall.

A little bead of sweat started to trickle down Ismael's forehead. He licked his lips. He bared his teeth.

'Twist,' he said.

Meanwhile, in *Sally's* mind . . .

'Trip her up!' howled Muddlespot, jumping up and down.

'No!' cried Windleberry.

'Jostle her!'

'No!'

'Swap her sugar for salt!'

'Nice one,' said Sally. But she went on working grimly.

'Now own up, children,' cried Mrs Bunnidy, a little less musically than before. 'Who threw that?'

And there was one other thing. It was a big one. As big as an elephant. In a way, it *was* an elephant.

When people talk about an 'elephant in the room', what they mean is that there's something really big that everyone knows and no one talks about. The elephant in this case was Mum. More exactly, it was Baking with Mum.

There was an elephant wandering around in the central chamber of Sally's mind. It was slightly floury, and in a funny way it did look a bit like Mum, which was odd because Mum didn't look like an elephant at all. But what it meant was what Baking with Mum meant.

It meant that Billie could shout, scream, manipulate, get her way, force people to do what she wanted just by making them sick of her, but she couldn't make herself good at baking. Being good at baking meant that you were patient. It meant that you paid attention. It meant that you didn't throw tantrums when you found that the lumps wouldn't come out of your dough – you just kept beating them until they did. You didn't go off stamping your feet and you did come and bake when Mum suggested it, and so you got a lot of practice. With Mum. Doing what Mum wanted.

If you were good at baking, it meant you were good with Mum. It meant that you were Good, full stop. You were what Mum wanted. There was nothing Billie could do about that.

And both girls knew it.

'Pass the milk,' said Sally quietly. Billie seemed not to hear.

'Pass the *milk*, please,' said Sally. Billie still seemed not to hear.

Sally walked round the back of Billie to reach the milk. Whereupon Billie passed it to where she had been standing.

'I had to get the goo off my fingers,' Billie said.

Howls broke out on the far side of the room, where a triple dough strike had just totalled a tray of raisins.

Sally looked at the pulsating mass in Billie's bowl. 'She said butterflies, not elephants.'

'Shud*dup!*'

*

'I don't know why I said that,' said Sally in her own mind. 'I must have elephants on the brain.'

(The elephant in Sally's brain reached a floury trunk over her shoulder and whipped one of the raw dough muffins from her tray.)

'Whoops!' came Billie's voice. The salt had somehow spilled over Sally's tray of muffins. 'Sorry.'

Thin smoke started coming out of the Inner Sally's ears.

'Don't react, Sally,' cried Windleberry, desperately hosing her down with the idea of a handy fire extinguisher. 'Don't *react!*'

'That's all right,' said the Inner Sally grimly.

'That's all right,' said the Outer Sally's voice.

'. . . I kept some extra back just in case . . .'

'. . . I kept some extra back just in case . . .'

'. . . You tried something like that,' the Inner Sally finished.

The Outer Sally left that bit unsaid.

Quickly Sally reshaped her spare dough into muffins while Billie looked daggers into her left ear. And deftly Sally opened the door of the preheated oven·

with one hand, and shoved her tray into the top spot. She checked the clock: fifteen minutes to lunch. Just nice.

Elsewhere around the room, chaos reigned. Amos was on his hands and knees coughing up half-digested batter. Kieran was feigning an epileptic fit in the corner. Flour dust hung like battle-smoke in the air.

'Children!' called Mrs Bunnidy. 'Time to start clearing up!'

Cries of pain greeted her words.

'If you *haven't* finished, you can let them bake over lunch. I will be here until quarter past. But all the ovens must be switched off by then. Is that clear?'

'Oh, Mrs *Bunnidy* . . . !'

'. . . But we have to get our *sandwiches*!'

'I've said all I'm going to say!' Even Mrs Bunnidy was beginning to crack. 'And *don't* forget to clear up!'

'I'm nearly finished,' said Billie stoutly. 'I'm definitely going to finish. They can do until I get back from lunch. Fresh muffins for pudding – yummy!'

Sally looked at the lumps of porridge-like dough on Billie's tray. She said nothing.

'But I'll have to make sure I'm first in the queue or they'll burn,' said Billie, putting them into the oven.

'Don't you dare leave me with your clearing—' Sally began.

'Just leave them to bake, right?' said Billie. 'Don't touch them.'

RIIIINNNGG!!! went the bell. At once, the sounds of a human avalanche began to rumble through the school.

'. . . At a *quarter* past, remember? And everything *must* be cleaned away, and *all* the surfaces wiped . . .'

'YIPPPEEE!' yelled Billie, disappearing into the general scrum of arms and legs at the exit, and leaving a moonscape of spilled flour, spilled egg, spilled egg mixed with flour and those little scraps of dough that are *really* difficult to get off once they've started to harden, uncleaned and unwiped on the work surface.

Sally stayed where she was, watching the clock.

After five more minutes she opened the oven door and took her own muffins out. She put them on the rack.

She picked up a cloth.

*

'Well, just look,' said Muddlespot in tones of surprise. 'She's left you to do all the clearing up.'

'I know,' said the Inner Sally.

She began to make wiping motions. As she did so something else sauntered into the chamber. It was an idea. The idea was a pressure gauge on legs. The needle was on the red.

'We have to let off steam,' said Muddlespot.

'No we don't,' said Windleberry. 'That's exactly what we don't have to do. We know why she did it . . .'

'Yes, we do,' said Sally.

'She was having trouble with her dough . . .'

'Mum makes dough,' said Sally. 'She's always ready for us to make it with her. That's how I learned. Billie could never be bothered.'

'Then let's just *leave* her share of the clearing up . . .'

'I'm not going to. I'm going to clean it up for her.'

'But *why*, Sally?'

'To show her what she is.'

'That's not a good answer, Sally.'

'Good?' cried Muddlespot. 'Just a moment! What do you mean, "good"?'

*

Sally finished wiping away all the mess. She tried one of her muffins. It tasted quite – well – quite nice, actually.

It was unnaturally quiet, now. The only other people in the room were Richard and David, who were clearing up the devastation left by the food-fight of the century. Mrs Bunnidy was standing over them. They were taking one hundred per cent of her attention. Sally could have lobbed fifty flour bombs behind Mrs Bunnidy's back, but she didn't. She waited.

She watched the clock.

After a little while, she ate another muffin. Somehow it didn't taste quite as good as the first.

'. . . And that's *always* the way, isn't it?' Muddlespot was working himself up into a frenzy. 'It's always *Sally* who has to clear up! It's always *Sally* who has to under-stand! It's always Sally who has to – er . . .'

'Make my bed,' said Sally.

'. . . Make her bed, and . . .'

'Practise my music.'

'. . . Practise her music, and . . .'

'Get the grades.'

'. . . Get the gr— Hang on! Who's tempting who here?'

163

'You're just so good at it, you see?' said Sally sweetly. 'But you left out the vegetables.'

'Vegetables?' said Windleberry.

'Billie makes a fuss about eating vegetables,' said Sally. 'So she gets small portions. I don't.'

'Isn't that *typical?*' cried Muddlespot. 'And why? Because Sally's good at everything! She's good at being good. *And everybody's got used to it!*'

'Don't listen to him, Sally!'

'I thought he was doing really well . . .'

Sally took another mouthful of muffin. She looked at the clock. Eight minutes past.

Carefully, she stowed her remaining muffins in an airtight Tupperware box.

She looked at the clock again. Still eight minutes past. Time was moving as slowly as a sandwich queue.

'There's no way she'll get back in time,' she said aloud. 'They'll just burn.'

'It's that or . . .'

She bent down.

'*No*, Sally!' cried Windleberry desperately. 'No, no, NO!'

Click, went the oven dial.

To '0'.

Somewhere, something else also went *click*.

To '1'.

On a scrap of paper Sally wrote, ***If you're hungry, you can have one of mine.*** She propped the note up by the Tupperware box.

She left the room.

15: NIGHTFALL

Muddlespot left the room too – the one in Sally's mind. He slipped quietly away around the statue of Reason. Behind him, Windleberry was protesting.

'You switched her oven off!'

'Yes,' said Sally.

'Her muffins will be spoiled!'

'They'd have been ruined anyway.'

Muddlespot tiptoed down the first set of stairs.

'You could have waited and taken them out . . .'

'Yeah. That's what *everybody* thinks I'll do.'

Muddlespot ran for it. He ran down corridors and across courts. He skittered past fountains and frowning statues. He found a series of narrow passages that he didn't remember (maybe they hadn't been there before) and he hurried down them. He came to a quiet corner where – unusually in Sally's mind – it was also rather dark.

He pulled out his communications dish and set it on its tripod. He scattered brown powder into the dish. He spat upon the powder.

Huff! it went, and burst into light.

Muddlespot waited, glancing nervously over his shoulder.

Slowly the flames died to embers. The embers faded from bright gold to orange, except for two spots like eyes that seemed to glow more brightly. The eyes fixed themselves on the little imp.

'Corozin here. Report, Muddlespot.'

Muddlespot gabbled out his story.

'You did what? I see. And did she …? Sssuper! You have done well, Muddlespot. I am pleased.'

'*Thank* you, Your Serenity!'

'Oh no. Thank you, Muddlespot. And …'

People say eyes smile. Eyes don't smile, because they don't have mouths to smile with. All that happens is that they change shape. Corozin's eyes changed shape now (they were just careful not to show their teeth).

'… Keep up the good work.'

*

'Yes!' cried Corozin gleefully, in his chamber of brass.

The glow in his communications dish was fading (taking the *ridiculous*, not to say *repulsive*, little face of Muddlespot with it). Quickly he conjured up more powder and scattered it over the embers. *Huff!* went the flames. Corozin leaned forward. His immaculate fingers were trembling with excitement.

There was the face of Sally Jones, looking calmly at him through the flames.

And there, written in figures of fire, was the LDC.

Lifetime Good Deeds: 3,971,756
Lifetime Bad Deeds: 1

'YES!' cried Corozin.

Breakthrough! At last! When everything else had failed!

'Switched off her sister's oven!' He chuckled. 'I like that . . .'

He always liked it when they played with fire.

'Guards!' he called. His voice flowed down the

corridors like lava down a mountainside. When he rose from his seat, all the palace trembled. And he stood before a mirror.

The figure in the mirror was beautiful. It smiled back at him. As he watched, the red robes it wore vanished, to be replaced by a dull red woolly jumper, artfully baggy and unravelling just a little at the elbow. And jeans, with the beginnings of a rip at one knee. He nodded. Yes, that would do.

'Guards!' he called again, and was answered by the distant rattle of knuckles along polished floors.

In the mirror, a red-brown scarf wove itself nonchalantly around his reflection's neck. Scuffed white trainers cloaked the hooves.

'Cool,' he said, experimentally.

The rattle of knuckles was coming closer.

Corozin stepped forward, into the mirror. At the same time his reflection stepped out to meet him. They seemed to blur into one another at the mirror's surface. When the guards entered, gawping, they found their master standing before them in a woolly jumper, scarf and jeans, while his red-robed reflection looked on benignly from the mirror.

'We are going up,' he said. 'To take charge.'

The guards looked at each other, and then at their lord.

'To take charge,' they answered dutifully.

(If in doubt, it was safest just to repeat what the boss had said. Even the hint of a question mark could have dire consequences. They had learned this from experience – mostly that of some of their former, less fortunate colleagues.)

'Of Things,' Corozin said.

He was not worried that the LDC registered only '1'. What mattered was that it registered anything at all. He knew, as well as any Archangel in Heaven, how enormous the possibilities were when someone who had been straight all along began for the first time to stray. Yes, he knew how to use shame. He knew how to make people hate themselves, and then how to use it when they did. He knew how to look for the little things, the things that didn't seem to matter at the time you did them.

He was particularly fond of the sort of little thing that, without anybody intending it, turned out to be very big afterwards. So big that nobody ever mentioned it, and nobody could ever forget it. Like causing damage to the house without meaning to. Or the maiming of a pet. Or the accidental death of a sister.

He had done it before.

Which left just one little problem. One little and rather warty problem. He knew the first question Low Command would ask when they heard the good news. It would be, 'Who had made the breakthrough?' And it would be unfortunate (not to say downright dangerous) for Corozin if the name they heard happened to be the wrong one.

But again, it wasn't the sort of problem that he couldn't solve. He'd had, after all, quite a lot of practice with this sort of problem recently. He twirled his brass hammer and smiled affectionately at his guards.

'I think our time has come.'

Some things just came naturally to Billie. She could achieve Modest Grades with No Effort in her sleep (and frequently did). She could achieve a Room so Untidy She Would Never Have to Clean It, with results that were truly impressive. And when she set out to Stir Up A Row, she was just world standard.

The aftermath of the Food Tech lesson, when the school authorities had woken up to the fact that the thing had been a complete disaster and were preparing to come down hard on anyone whose name got mentioned in connection with it, gave her the perfect opportunity.

'*Sally!*' said Mrs Bunnidy, who had been hauled along the corridor by a red-faced Billie. 'Is this true? *Did* you switch off Billie's oven?'

'Yes, I did,' said Sally.

She forbore to remind Mrs Bunnidy that she had said all ovens had to be off by a quarter past. She also did not bother to say that the forlorn and lumpy set of half-baked muffins Billie had tearfully produced as Exhibit A were about averagely good for Billie's baking. Had she switched off the oven? She had. Had she meant to spoil Billie's muffins? She had. Guilty as charged.

'*Well!*' cried Mrs Bunnidy. 'I'm – I'm shocked, Sally. Shocked and disappointed. I don't know what to say. You'll have to see your Head of Year . . .'

Sally said nothing.

'. . . *Well!*' said Mr Singh, Head of Year. 'Sally, I'm surprised at you! Surprised and disappointed. We expect pupils in this school to respect each other. Do you have anything to say?'

Sally said nothing. There was no point.

172

'You will join Richard and David and Charlie B in detention. And before the next Food Tech period I am going to speak with the whole class. The general level of behaviour was disgraceful.'

Still Sally said nothing, though maybe she went a little pale. She had never, ever had a detention before. She had never, ever been bracketed with boys like Richard and David or even Charlie B.

And detention, she realized, meant she would get home late.

Billie would get there first.

With her muffins.

'*Sally!*' cried Mum that evening. 'I – I don't know what to say. That was just – *spiteful*! Wasn't it? I'm – I'm *very* disappointed . . .'

Sally stood in the hallway with her bag over one shoulder. The bag was heavy. Her shoes and tights were wet from coming home in the latest shower of rain, and her knee was scraped and sore and still throbbing slightly from when she had fallen on the hockey pitch. Still she didn't say anything. But maybe her face hardened a little. Maybe she let her eyes say a little of what she felt.

And Mum, tired, dismayed, bewildered, lost it.

'*Don't* be like that with me! You *never* give Billie a chance! You *never* let her get it right! What's the matter with you? You don't do *anything* to help her . . . '

Pale-faced, Sally stood it for about eight seconds. Then she turned for the stairs.

'*Go* to your room!' said Mum hurriedly, before Sally could hit the first step with a stomp. 'Go to your room! And don't come down until you can be *nice* to your sister!'

Sally did not stomp. She just climbed the stairs.

'She – (sob) – ruined my – *muffins!*' Billie wailed.

'Never mind, sweetheart,' Sally heard Mum say. '*We* can make some more. Would you like that?'

'It won't be the *sa-a-a-ame!*' cried Billie.

'Look, I was going to bake something later anyway. You can help me. And you can lick the bowl afterwards.'

'Sniff,' said Billie.

Sally closed her bedroom door.

The evening drew on. Shadows fell around the Jones

household. Other shadows moved within them.

'No Sally?' said Greg at supper.

'She's having a sulk,' said Billie.

'*Sally's* having a sulk?' said Greg, incredulous.

In the hallway, Shades tensed. His eyes narrowed.

'. . . So I sent her upstairs,' said Mum. 'And she's decided to stay there. It's a battle of wills, I suppose.'

'Well done,' said Greg.

'Are we going to do those muffins now?' asked Billie hopefully.

'In a moment, sweetheart. We'll start them tonight and have them for breakf— Oh.' She turned to Greg. 'Did you call the electrician?'

'Er . . . no. I was going to . . .'

'Uuuurgh!' groaned Mum in despair. 'Can't you do *anything*? One day we're going to wake up with the house on fire!'

'Ovens are metal,' said Greg reasonably. 'Even if something burns, there's not too much that can go wrong as long as you don't open the oven door.'

Billie, with some effort, was persuaded to go and stack the dishwasher. While she was clattering in the kitchen, Mum put her head in her hands.

'I didn't handle it well,' she said. 'I just wasn't *ready* for it. I got home shattered . . .'

'Never mind,' said Greg.

'. . . Billie was so upset. She's like me. She takes everything to heart. She doesn't react well when things go wrong for her . . .'

'*You* were never like that?' said Greg, his eyes widening diplomatically.

'All the time. I still am a bit, aren't I?'

'Mmm,' said Greg, again diplomatically.

'Sally's got to learn that the world's not perfect. It's never going to be. She can't expect it to be . . .'

'Mmm.'

'She gets *that* from her father.'

Greg nodded wisely.

'Damn him,' said Mum.

'Mmm.'

'He was a sock fascist.'

'Mmm.'

'Don't keep saying "mmm".'

'What do you want me to say?'

*

Ismael looked up to call for his card. But for once Scattletail was not watching him.

He was looking away at the twin windows on the world. At the lights of the kitchen, where the Outer Billie worked, humming, on her dough. He was looking at the shadows beyond the light.

'What's up?' asked Ismael.

'Felt something,' said Scattletail.

Ismael waited. Scattletail just sat there. He sat very, very still.

'Twist,' said Ismael eventually.

Scattletail glanced down at the pack. He seemed to have forgotten all about it. He flipped a card to Ismael and went back to watching the shadows.

The card was the three of hearts. With his six and eight, that made seventeen. 'Stick,' said Ismael.

Scattletail glanced at the pack again. He turned three cards in quick succession, barely looking at them. 'Bank's bust,' he said. 'C'mon. Let's go for a walk.'

Ismael blinked at the fallen cards. Scattletail should never have turned that last one. He had made nineteen without it. 'Why did you do that?' he demanded.

'Dunno. Must've been thinking 'bout something else. You coming?'

'Hey! I *won*. It's my shout, right?'

Scattletail glanced at Billie, who had her back to them. He shrugged. 'Sure. Go ahead.'

'Hey, Bills,' said Ismael. 'What say we make an extra one for Sally in the morning? Kind of a peace offering?'

'Awww!' moaned Billie.

'Just to watch her face when she sees it,' Ismael wheedled. 'Guess her jaw will drop a mile, right?'

'Guess it'll come off its hinges,' said Billie.

Scattletail was waiting at the door. 'Nice one,' he said. 'You ready?'

'Sure. Where are we going?'

'Out.'

'*Out?* What for?'

'Just for a walk. Oh – you still got that fiddle o' yours?'

Ismael blinked again. His 'fiddle' – his Celestial Gladivarius violin with its bow of finest spider's silk – was propped in the back of the cupboard in his room and buried under thirteen years' worth of copy reports. He hadn't taken it out since the very early days.

'Yeah. Think so. Why?'

Scattletail breathed a gout of yellow smoke. 'Do a spot of busking, maybe. You never know.'

Busking? thought Ismael.

Outside?

Outside was the human world. Humans didn't hear angelic music – not like that. Not without serious and highly dubious forms of stimulation. There'd be no one out there to listen except angels, demons and the cat. And none of *them* would be paying. Not to hear Scattletail sing, at any rate.

They might pay him to stop.

'Muddlespot.'

Muddlespot started. It *can't* be, he thought.

Here?

Soft-footed, he hurried down a passage in Sally's mind. He looked around.

Nothing.

'Muddlespot,' came the voice again.

It *sounded* like . . . With an ugly feeling, Muddlespot followed it. He didn't want to have to talk to Corozin again – largely because he had already given all the good news he had to give, and there were one or two things about the way things were here (Windleberry, for example) that were not such good news and that he didn't want to have to explain about.

One or two things. By the time he reached the end of the corridor he had counted about eighteen. And as for excuses, he was stuck on three.

'Muddlespot.'

Panting, he passed under an arch into a six-sided chamber. In the middle of the chamber was a crystal statue with its arm pointing. There was no one else.

'Er . . . did you speak?' said Muddlespot, feeling foolish.

'Nope,' said a voice behind him. 'That was us.'

Two huge green leathery claws landed on his shoulders. He felt himself being plucked up off his feet. He looked into the grinning faces of Corozin's two guards.

'Sur-*prise!*'

'Eeeeeeeeeeeeeeeek!' said Muddlespot.

'Pleased to see us?' leered one.

'Poor Muddlespot!' said the other. 'Up here in the big world, and all on his own.'

'Er . . . are you staying long?' asked Muddlespot, trembling with shock.

'Oh no, Muddlespot! Just accompanying the boss on his rounds.'

'I see,' said Muddlespot, who for some reason was trembling even more.

'Oh yes. He's got something for you. Something *good*.'

'Er . . . good?'

The guards' eyes gleamed.

'A *reward*, Muddlespot. For being *such* a special agent.'

'Come this way.'

Still gripping him firmly by the elbows, they steered him across the chamber towards the outer passage.

'But – but my post! I can't leave my post!'

His legs were no longer dangling. They were bicycling. Unfortunately they were still in the air.

'Oh don't *worry*, Muddlespot!' said one cheerfully.

'The boss will take care of it,' grinned the other. 'The boss will take care of *everything*.'

*

Windleberry tried again.

'Sally, look,' he said. 'What's happened? Three grown-ups who don't know everything that happened have shouted at you. That's all, isn't it? Why does it matter so much?'

'It's not that,' said Sally.

In the outer world, she was sitting on her bed with her arms tightly folded. She had switched her light off and got into her pyjamas. She wasn't going to sleep. In fact, she didn't think she would sleep at all. But she didn't want anyone coming in. Not even to say good night.

'I can't put a foot wrong,' she said. 'I'm not *allowed* to.'

'Sally . . .'

She folded her arms even more tightly. A series of shapes and ideas danced through the room. Windleberry watched them grimly. Some of them were rimmed with fire.

'You can send them away,' he said.

She shrugged. 'All right.'

They left.

But they didn't go far. All down the corridors of Sally's mind there was a low murmuring. Windleberry could feel it, like something crawling on his skin. In their separate rooms the ideas were pacing, muttering to themselves like prisoners before a riot. They knew something was up. Some of them were frightened. Some were fierce. It sounded as though a fight was starting down in the History cells.

And there was a peculiar colour to the air. Orange or orange-red, like a fiery sunset – or maybe just a fire. It was almost as if he were watching Sally through tinted glass, except that it was misty rather than glassy. Red mist. Windleberry had heard of it. He had not seen it from the inside before.

'Sally,' he said. 'It wasn't really *you* the grown-ups were stressed about. You weren't the main trouble in that classroom. That was the boys. And you aren't the top worry on your mum's mind . . .'

'No,' said Sally grimly.

'But maybe I should be,' she added.

'What . . . ?'

'I said, maybe I should be. Maybe she should worry about me more than she does.'

'*Sally!*'

She looked up at him. He looked into her eyes.

There was something wrong. Something inside

183

the Inner Sally. There were *two* pairs of eyes, looking at him from her face. Sally's, and . . .

A horrible, cold prickling feeling stole over Windleberry's skin. His jaw clenched.

'Come out,' he said.

It was as if he had a moment of double vision. First there was just Sally. And then a shape that was almost Sally's shape separated from her – a head, a pair of shoulders, a body lounging easily just to the left of where Sally sat bolt upright with her arms folded tightly across her chest.

It was a man – a very beautiful man. He wore a woolly jumper, a scarf, jeans and branded trainers. He might have been lounging on the back page of a fashion magazine.

Except for his eyes.

'Get away from her,' said Windleberry softly.

Still smiling, the man rose. He strolled away to where the statue of Wizdum slouched over its electric guitar. He smiled. Then he breathed on it.

Very slowly, the statue drooped, as if it were made of melted ice cream. Its robe dribbled down into a shapeless mass around its waist and knees. The face crumpled from young smooth skin into a hideous, sagging drool.

The Enemy looked at it, critically. 'Just speeding things up,' he said.

How did he do it? thought Windleberry. *How did he get in here – get this close, without me knowing?*

This wasn't any of the ordinary scum. He knew that. He could feel it.

This was someone Big. Ancient.

Evil.

Windleberry sprang between Sally and the Enemy, arms up, knees flexed, body balanced to spring forward or back. The Enemy looked at him. His smile broadened, a little.

'Oh, my hero,' it said.

'I can take you, fiend.'

'No weapons? Not even a tin whistle, I think. Shame.'

'With my eyes and with my hands,' said Windleberry. 'One on one.'

'Ah, but you see . . .'

'. . . I'm not alone,' Corozin finished, as Windle-berry crumpled to the floor.

Sally stood over him, with a little brass hammer in her hand.

16: THE REWARD

'That was cool,' said the man.

'I had to hit *something*,' said Sally. 'He was just nearest.'

'Remind me not to turn my back on you.'

'Don't. I'm in a mean mood.' She looked at the hammer in her hand. 'Is this yours?'

'I've several. What's mine is yours, etcetera. But next time, try giving it a bit more welly. You'd be surprised what that thing can do when you really let yourself go.'

He looked around the crystal chamber. He studied the long, transparent corridors, the colours pulsing delicately in the walls. 'Nice place. Well looked after.'

'Thanks.'

'Ah.' He had seen the little door. 'Very convenient. Normally you have to go hunting about among all the lumber.'

'There's no lumber here.'

'No?' He opened the low door. Beyond it was the little room with the trap door. Neatly wound around the catch was the bright little wire of Swiftness, connecting the batteries of Virtue to the primer of Decision and the tubes of Pure Distilled Truth.

'Did you want that lot there?'

'Not much,' said Sally, studying it. 'What's it for?'

'It's just a little check on your freedom. Entirely well-meant, of course.'

'Get rid of it,' said Sally.

Deftly he plucked the batteries of Virtue from the circuit. He opened the hatch. Nothing happened. Windleberry's device lay dead on the floor at his feet. Carefully he picked up the glistening amber tubes, with the wire and the rest of it dangling from them. Still nothing happened. He too knew about Truth and how to use it (in his case, very sparingly). He dropped them down the hatch.

Sally came and stood over the void. She looked down into it. She waited.

No sound came.

'We could drop the stiff down there too. Stop him being a pain, if you like.'

Sally looked into the void. She heard whispers, and felt a gentle updraught of warm air. She shook her head. 'He's part of me. Same as you.'

'He's not going to be pleased when he comes round . . .'

'We'll tie him up. I've got my old bonds somewhere. We can use those.'

He shrugged. 'You're the boss,' he said.

She studied him curiously. 'Where's the other one? The little bloke?'

'Muddlespot?' Corozin smiled. He shook his head gently. 'He's gone out. He'll be . . . Maybe he'll be a little while.'

'Er, this reward,' said Muddlespot, a little nervously. 'Is it, um, a full-sized set of horns?'

They were making their way along the broad ridge that was Sally's shoulder, one guard ahead, one behind.

'Nope,' said the guard ahead. 'Guess again.'

'Is it demotion?'

(In Pandemonium, demotion – implying a movement downwards – is very much preferred to the alternative.)

'Ah,' said the guard. 'Ah, yes. Sort of.'

'But you have to guess what *kind* of demotion,' said the other one. 'That's it, isn't it?'

'Here we are,' said the first, as Sally's shoulder sloped sharply downwards before his feet. 'Jump.'

They grabbed Muddlespot by both elbows and launched themselves into the air.

Quite a long time later, they landed on Sally's bedside table. Muddlespot, who had shut his eyes, went flat on his face. 'Ow,' he said.

'Quick. Let's not hang about,' said a guard. They hauled Muddlespot to his feet and scuttled for the shelter of the lamp stand.

'This'll do,' said one, looking around.

'Right, Muddlespot. You stand there. Shut your eyes. When I count to three, you open them. Right?'

'Er, right,' said Muddlespot, covering his eyes. 'Do I get another guess?'

'*Last* guess, Muddlespot. And no peeking.'

'One!'

'By the grace of His Majesty, the Prince of all

190

Pandemonium, the Son of the Morning, the Lord of the Low, etcetera, we his servants—'

'Is it the key to my own palace?' said Muddlespot.

'Is it the key to his palace? That's *close*, Muddle-spot. That's *very* close. Two!'

'. . . Hereby bestow thee, Muddlespot, Wartspawn, Slugtrail, Agent a Little Bit Worthy—'

'Three!'

'. . . With thy duly merited reward. Look up, Muddlespot!'

Muddlespot looked up. Over him hovered a huge brass hammer. It filled the sky.

They held it poised over his head.

'Good night, Muddlespot!'

Grinning . . .

The hammer coming down . . .

It seemed to move so slowly. So slowly. And Muddlespot could not move at all. He could not think.

He shut his eyes.

'ZINGA-ZINGA-ZINGZINGA-ZING!!!'

THUD!!!

He opened his eyes.

The hammer was lying before him. Flat on its side, it came about up to his waist. Not that he had a waist, but he had an upper part of his body which got bigger as it went down, and then a lower part of his body that got smaller as it went down, and then he had his legs. What's more, all of it was still attached to him.

Smattered and scattered in a wide circle around the hammer were the remains of the two guards. They had been torn to pieces: shot full of holes. The holes were shaped like little musical notes.

'Thanks, Ismael,' said Scattletail, who was lounging by the lamp stand. Beside him, clutching a smoking violin, was an angel. 'Nice shooting. We owe you one.'

'OK,' said the angel. 'So: Billie does the washing up – without being asked?'

Scattletail seemed to hesitate for a moment. Then he said, 'Sure. Go ahead. Me an' the kid here're gonna have a chat.'

'Take your time,' said the angel. 'Don't hurry back.' He jumped off the table and disappeared.

'But . . . but . . .' said Muddlespot dazedly.

'Take it easy.'

'You're with *them*? The Other Side?'

'Nope.'

Muddlespot stared at the remains of the fallen guards. 'They were going to smash me,' he said.

'Yep.'

'But I was doing what I was *supposed* to!'

'Yep.'

'And you got that . . .'

'Fluffy?'

'He . . .'

'He did me a favour. We've known each other a while, kid. It gets like that. C'mon. Let's walk.'

He led the way to the edge of the table and slid down the lamp flex. Muddlespot followed. He caught up with Scattletail on the carpet.

'But – the *War*!' he said desperately.

'No compromise, huh? No meeting place?'

'It's . . . not allowed,' said Muddlespot. He felt quite weak.

Scattletail ambled on ahead of him, hands in his pockets. The spaces of Sally's room were huge around

193

him. 'Ever look at a human war, kid? No? Very instructive. *Ve*-ry instructive. You get two sides going at each
other. Just like us. It's 'bout places, mostly. Most human
wars're 'bout places. And both sides're told it's a fight
to the finish. No meeting place, etcetera. That's what
they say . . .

'But what they *do's* a bit different. *OK*, they
think. *You want that place real bad. We won't fight
you for it. Not yet. You keep that place, right. We'll
keep this one. Let's not make too much trouble. Too
many of us might get hurt.* Most of the time it's like
that. Sometimes they even kick a football around.
Sometimes a boss on one side says to a boss on the
other, "Hey, pal. I sent some guys over to your side some
days back. What happened? They're all dead? Sure.
Only I got to tell the families, see . . ." It happens, kid.
Most of the time they're only fighting just enough to
keep the fight going. Mostly they're leaving each other
alone. Trying to keep the holes in their pants down
to four.'

Dazed, Muddlespot struggled to understand. Wars.
Places. Humans. Holes. Pants . . .

Pants with *four* holes.

One for each leg, he thought. One for the waist,
three . . .

Oh, most of them would be male. Right.

So that made four. Got that. So . . .

'But *then*,' grunted Scattletail. 'Then what happens is someone – usually some boss – thinks, OK, you *want that place real bad. So* we'll *take it. We'll take it to show you we can. We'll take it to show you we're winning. That'll be good, won't it? Then* you see two sides kicking the stuff out of each other. Bleeding real bad. For what? For a place. A hill. Something that once was a town. Nothing that'll be worth what it's costing them by the time they've finished. Just a place. Or in our case, it might be a kid.'

They passed under Sally's door. The landing was in half-light. Voices rose up the stairs. Greg was watching television. Billie and her mum were in the kitchen, humming as they worked together.

'Darlington Row,' said Scattletail. 'As normal as it comes. We ship some out, they ship some out. Fair enough. But as long as they had Sally, and we were getting nowhere near her, they could reckon they were ahead. Low Command didn't like that. That's why someone in Low Command's said "Take that kid". Who did they say it to? Corozin.'

'But I was getting her!' wailed Muddlespot. 'Or at least,' he added, with the ingrained honesty of a cleaner

195

who every day has to admit to himself that he hasn't *quite* removed that stain yet, 'I'd made a start.'

'Sure. But what did that look like to Corozin? Remember how Corozin got his place? By looking smarter than his boss. So his boss was hauled down to Low Command and went under the hammer, and Corozin got the palace. Now Corozin's using up agents like coal on a fire and still getting nowhere with Sally, and Low Command's getting sick about it. Who're they getting sick with? Corozin. What happens if Low Command thinks there's an agent up here – one who's finally started to get somewhere with their precious kid – who might be smarter than Corozin . . . ? But if Corozin can make it look like *he's* done what's needed, maybe he'll be moving into a bigger palace, lower down the hill. See?'

'How do you know all this?'

'He's a devil, ain't he?'

'Well yes . . .'

'I know the type.'

From down below came the splosh of water. It sounded like water in a bucket. Billie was still humming.

'I wonder,' sighed Muddlespot, peering through the banisters of the Joneses' stairwell. 'If there's a vacancy for a cleaner anywhere round here. Nice long hours, low pay – or none at all . . .'

'You can't run from Corozin, kid. As long as you're around, he's not going to feel safe. It's you or him.'

'Me?'

Against Corozin?

A thought popped into Muddlespot's head. Or maybe it exploded.

It was:

HEEEEEEELLPPPPP!!!

'Help,' he said feebly.

Voices rose from below.

'Billie, what . . . are you mopping the floor?'

'Thought it needed it,' said Billie brightly.

'Yes . . . yes . . .' For a moment Mum seemed to be lost for words. 'Thank you, sweetheart. That's *really* good of you . . .'

'I'd spilled a bit,' Billie confessed.

'I give Ismael an inch,' sighed Scattletail, 'an' he takes a freakin' mile.'

'Help,' murmured Muddlespot. In his mind, the mop had become a brass brush and pan and was busy sweeping up fragments of Muddlespot.

'I left the muffins in the fridge. We can bake them in the morning and have them fresh for breakfast.'

'If there's time . . .'

'And I've tidied up the spice cupboard, Mum . . .'

'Right,' said Scattletail. 'That does it – I've got to get back. Things are getting *way* out of hand down there.'

'Help me!' said Muddlespot.

Scattletail looked at him. 'I already did, didn't I?'

'But I can't take Corozin on my own!'

'Nor can I, kid. Did you think I could?'

'But . . .'

'Look, kid, I'm glad to do what I can. I don't want *him* up here near me any more than you do. But I got to look after myself. Anyway, what goes on in there . . .' He jerked his thumb back at Sally. 'I can't be getting into that. Not my territory. That's got to be between you and him. And her. See?'

'Yes,' said Muddlespot heavily. 'I see.'

Deep within the hard, cold eyes of Scattletail there was a gleam of regret. 'Good luck, kid,' he said. 'And think – holes in pants.'

'Yeah, I know,' Muddlespot sighed. 'Keep them to five.'

17: HELP

Sally wasn't used to talking about herself. It wasn't something she did much. Mostly she listened to her friends talking about *them*selves, and she would say the things they needed to hear. The important thing was to be interested.

Until now, she'd had most of the stuff about herself already sorted. So what would have been the point of talking about it?

But that wasn't true any more.

And now that she had stuff she wanted to say — things that if they *didn't* get out through her mouth would swell up and make her chest burst — she didn't know how to say them. She stumbled. She put her hand to her head and said, 'No, that's not right. What

I *meant* was . . .' She shook her fists and paced up and down like a starlet in a TV soap, or like Cassie complaining about the latest man she had ditched. She knew it was acting. She knew that half of it wasn't real. She just didn't know how else to do it.

Anyway, he seemed interested.

'All this "Being Good" – it's been a con,' she said. 'A great big *con*. And I fell for it.'

He put his head on one side. He didn't question what she meant by '*all this Being Good*'. And she was glad, because she would have found that difficult to answer without saying something really tacky like 'Everything' or 'My Life', etcetera.

He asked: 'Who's been conning you?'

Sally faced him. 'I have,' she said.

She thought about how deep his eyes were. They seemed to know a lot more than he said. Sometimes she wondered if he knew what she was going to say before she did.

'And . . . ?'

She shrugged. 'And everybody else has got used to it.'

'Why?'

'Because it suits them.'

'It does, doesn't it?'

Help, thought Muddlespot.

He was cowering in the shelter of the banisters, wondering if there was anywhere better to hide. Anywhere Corozin wouldn't find him.

The huge figure of Mum was climbing up the stairs before his eyes. She was calling over her shoulder, 'Billie, bedtime!'

'Coming,' answered Billie's voice from below.

On Mum's shoulder two tiny figures circled, throwing punches at each other and emitting squeaks of rage. One had white wings and a halo. The other had horns and a tail.

Help, thought Muddlespot. If I'm seen. If it gets back to Corozin where I am . . . How long before he finds out what happened to his guards?

He scuttled round to the other side of the banister. He almost ran into a face.

It was a huge face, black, yellow eyed, furry, topped with two enormous triangular ears.

'HEEEELP!' screamed Muddlespot.

In the black face a little line parted. It opened into a mouth the size of a volcano cone, edged with huge pale teeth and floored with a vast pink tongue.

What kind of help, exactly? said the cat with a yawn.

It didn't actually speak. No words travelled through the air. But its meaning was (ahem) purrfectly clear.

'Er . . .' said Muddlespot, still trembling with the shock. 'Any, really. Any at all.'

I see.

'Er, yes! Yes you can!' agreed Muddlespot. 'I – er – that is, you *can* see me. How do you do that?'

The cat blinked, hugely.

You can't be a figment of my imagination, it said. *I don't have one.*

'No, I – er – you said you could help me?'

Shades studied the tiny imp. It made him look cross-eyed.

Possibly, he said at last.

'Thank you! Oh, thank you!'

. . . For a price.

'Name it – anything! Anything!'

You have to bow down and worship me.

'I beg your . . . WHAT??!!???' shrieked Muddlespot.

You have a problem with this?

'But – but – it's the wrong way round! It's supposed to be the other way around!'

Take it or leave it, buster.

Angels don't often get headaches. They don't drink. They don't suffer from migraines. They do play music, sometimes quite loud music, but it doesn't generally have that sort of effect.

So for Windleberry, coming round with a head like the insides of Krakatoa was a new experience. And it wasn't interesting.

It was even less interesting to discover that he was tied to a chair, with ropes around his wrists, ankles and arms all pulled so tight that he might have been cased in concrete. He had cramp in about six different places and it hurt like . . .

Like the other place.

His mouth was filled with cloth. A gag. It forced his jaw wide open and was tied firmly at the back of his head. If it had been stuffed any further down his throat, he'd have had to swallow it. He could hear voices, but somehow they didn't seem very important. What was important was the headache, the cramp and the gag. He hated all of them. In that order.

Or maybe the cramps were worst. They made him want to scream.

Or maybe it was the gag. Because it meant he couldn't.

There were two voices. Sally's was one.

'I shouldn't have walked away. I just couldn't handle it. Mum shouting at me like that. I should have stayed and told them what I thought.'

'That would have been better.'

'I just can't *complain*! It's not something I do. So they think I'll take it. They think I'll *always* take it. It's because I'm *always* making room for them. In the end, I've no place left for myself. They've got to make some space for me too.'

'They've left you out, haven't they?'

'I've got to show them . . . '

'What have you got to show them?'

' . . . That I can't be pushed.'

Windleberry gathered his strength, like a long intake of breath. Then, on a command from his brain, all his muscles jerked violently.

Nothing.

He could not move against the bonds. Not a finger, and not so much as a hair's-breadth. They were Sally's

205

bonds, and this was Sally's mind. She could keep him like this just as long as she wanted to.

Oh, Sally, please . . . he thought.

The view through the windows had changed. The Outer Sally had got out of bed. She was standing in the middle of her room. The Inner Sally was standing too. Her fists were clenched.

'Mum's so desperate about Billie that she'll scream at me just to show Billie she's being fair.'

'So she screamed at you to make things better between her and Billie?'

Sally nodded slowly.

'So she was never going to listen to you anyway. Because . . .'

'Because she—'

'Wants you to be . . .'

'Wants me . . .' said Sally slowly.

(*No, Sally! No!* thought Windleberry desperately.)

'. . . To be the bad one,' said Sally.

Silence.

'Ouch,' said Sally.

She was crying.

'Crazy, isn't it?' said the man. 'All that trying.

Even tying yourself up. And all it takes is one click of an oven switch, and suddenly you see what's been there all along.'

'Yeah,' said Sally.

'Of course, if you had *really* been the bad one, she'd have got more than she bargained for.'

'Yeah, she would.'

'Tantrums are just stupid.'

'They make you look like a kid.'

'But little things. At the right time. Just to show her what she's wished on herself.'

'Like?'

'Like – oh, the click of an oven switch, maybe.'

Sally hesitated. 'Now?' she asked.

The man shrugged. 'Well, they complained when you switched it *off*, didn't they?'

'Burn the muffins?'

'Do you like the smell of burning?'

'I don't know. It depends.'

'I do.'

The mind of a cat is quite different.

It does have rooms – a few. They don't have signs on them, because the cat doesn't need them. It knows perfectly well that *that* one is the room where it keeps the idea 'Wash', and *that's* the one where it keeps the idea 'Lap', and *that's* where it keeps the (very over-worked) idea 'Eat'. There's also 'Find Sunny Spot', 'Kill It', 'Can't Be Bothered', and maybe one or two others. At most.

There aren't any corridors. The doors of these rooms all open directly onto the central chamber. And they aren't doors, of course – they're cat flaps. Except for the 'Eat' one, which has come off its hinges from overuse.

There are no strange noises, no nightmares, no guilty thoughts chained to the walls. In the mind of the cat, guilt does not exist. There is no trap door.

Nor are there any fountains, decorations, statues, no ideals. That's because . . .

. . . In the central chamber . . .

(Which is huge, by the way. *Probably* it's domed, but it's a little hard to tell because cats aren't much interested in architecture.)

. . . Is the Cat Itself.

It is enormous. It is majestic. Its head is the size of the night sky and its eyes are like twin yellow moons. It is like the vast statues in ancient temples built by thousands of sweating slaves to honour a god. Which is what all cats are – in their own minds.

The great face leered down upon Muddlespot.

Feast your eyes, Mister, the cat said.

Windleberry jerked at his bonds. Nothing.

Mustn't panic! he thought.

Must. Not . . .

Now!

Again he jerked, begging for just that slight loosening that could be the start of a struggle for freedom. There was nothing. He was held fast.

The windows on the outer world showed a view of the stairs in darkness. Sally was standing at the top of them. All the lights down there were off. Everyone was in bed. Only the pervasive yellow glow of the streetlights, filtering in through cracks in curtains and the little window above the door, lit the outlines of the banisters, steps and object-cluttered hall. It was like looking down from a great height into darkness and seeing a city far below. A city built, perhaps, of brass.

And the unsettled murmurs ran down the corridors of Sally's mind. A low, background humming. Ominous.

The Inner Sally stood before her windows. She was still in her pyjamas. The man in the red-brown scarf stood beside her. He had a friendly hand upon her shoulder.

Sweat gathered on Windleberry's forehead. It was a trick – he knew it.

Ovens are metal. Greg had said it. All the family knew it. Even if something burned inside them, nothing could really go wrong as long as you didn't open the door.

But ovens aren't just metal. They have wires, trim and other parts. If it's a cheap double oven, with wires that run close to the oven casing . . . If it's turned on and left on, while everyone's in bed. If the thermostat fails so that the heat builds and builds . . . Old fat. Spilled grease on the elements. Lint and crumbs and other stuff that's fallen down the cracks around and behind the cooker, because this is the Jones household and the cleaning's always been a bit haphazard . . .

There would be a fire. Damage – something Sally never intended. Something that she'd get blamed for.

And then there would be guilt. And her anger that she was being made to feel guilty; at the unfairness of it. The Enemy could work on that. Like feeding a fire, bit by bit, until the first small spark had become a terrible thing, burning within her.

All those fingers pointing at her. *You* were the one who started it, they would say. It was your fault. And even if they didn't say it, she would feel them thinking it. And Billie – Billie would never let her forget it.

If Billie survived . . .

The thought was like a trap door opening in the bottom of his soul.

An enemy like this did not bother with the little things. He was going for the big one. Now, when things had barely begun. When no one imagined that it could happen.

Sally was moving down the stairs. Softly, in darkness. And in her mind the murmurs were rising like a low wind. Windleberry thought he could hear screams.

18: YOU ARE IN MY POWER

The bonds held him fast. Because she wanted them to.

Oh, Sally, he thought.

She was in the hall. Looking into the kitchen.

Oh, Sally. Give me a chance!

'They're in the fridge,' Sally said.

'Just slip them into the oven,' said the man. 'And set it to – oh, to maximum. Why not?'

The fridge door was open. The tray was in her hands.

Oh, Sally, please . . .

'Miiiaaaow!'

It was a pitiful little noise. Plaintive. From down at Sally's feet.

'What?' said Sally.

'What . . . ?'

A face was looking up from the kitchen floor. Black, yellow eyed, pointy eared. Pathetic.

'What's the matter, puss?' said Sally.

From down below, she seemed like a mountain. Her face was as high as the clouds. But Muddlespot, squinting upwards through the cat's eyes, saw all the way to hers. He saw in them a look he knew.

'There's Corozin!' he said urgently, tugging at the paw of the huge Inner Cat beside him. 'Attack! You've got to attack!'

Wrong idea, buster . . . said the cat drily.

'Aaaaaooooww?' went the Outer Cat. It was such a piteous sound.

'Poor puss,' said Sally. 'Has no one fed you?'

Yeah, about that, said the Inner Cat sourly. *Did you know that someone's been spitting in my dish?*

But Shades was an old hand. He was a pro. Not for a moment did he let his attention wander. He looked up at her, eyes big, mouth small, all purpose and focus and pure intent, doing what a cat does best. Muddle-spot, watching from the vantage of the cat's brain, was filled with admiration.

'You can't have these,' said Sally, looking at the tray in her hands. 'They're . . .'

Her voice trailed away. She went on looking at the muffins.

'Aaaaaooooww,' went the cat again.

Look at me. Pity me.

Pity me, a poor, lonesome, half-starved puss. Forget everything else. Forget your sister. Forget your mother. Here, in the empty night, there is only pitiful me.

Look. Pity Me. Love Me.

You are in my power.

Something that was tight around Windleberry's hand seemed to twitch. And it wasn't so tight any more.

'In the *oven*,' hissed the Enemy. 'You were putting them in the *oven*!'

'Wait,' sighed Sally.

She put down the tray. She picked up the cat. She was thinking, as she lifted him, I know your game, Shades. Attention. That's all you want. You're a heartless, selfish beast. You'll take it from anyone who'll give it to you. But you're warm and you're furry and – I could do with a cuddle.

'Poor puss,' she said, holding his face right close to hers, so they touched at the nose. 'It's the middle of the night, isn't it? What are we doing here?'

Windleberry could move his elbow. An inch more . . .

Corozin saw in the cat's eyes a look he knew.

'MUDDLESPOT?' He leaned out through Sally's eyes. He leaned in through the cat's. He thrust his face into Muddlespot's face, right close so that their noses touched. 'WHAT are you doing here?!?'

'Er . . . talking to you?' simpered Muddlespot.

Corozin's arm joined his face in the cat's inner chamber. In his fist he held his huge brass hammer. 'Prepare to be horribly smashed into horrible little pieces!' he hissed.

'Look behind you,' said Muddlespot, grinning.

And Windleberry, bonds loosed, flew from his chair. 'FIEND!' he roared. 'FACE THE WRATH OF HEAVEN!'

19: THE WRATH OF HEAVEN

Part 1

It was cold in the kitchen. Especially around her neck and wrists and ankles.

ZAP!

Still holding the cat to her shoulder, Sally opened the fridge door with her foot. With one hand, she slid the tray of muffins back where they belonged. She wasn't really thinking about it. It was just her body doing what it always did – putting things back where they should be.

She stood in the middle of the kitchen, feeling the empty, dazed wrongness of being upright in the middle of the night.

Somehow it was hard to think.

20: THE WRATH OF HEAVEN

Part 2

Down came the hammer again. Windleberry back-flipped, picked up the statue of Trufe and flung it at his oncoming foe.

SMASH!

'*Hey!*' said the Inner Sally.

Brass and crystal exploded together in a cloud of shimmering dust. Corozin stumbled forward, wiping his eyes. Fragments of crystal smouldered, embedded in his skin like thorns. 'You will pay for this!' he snarled.

'Hey,' said the Inner Sally. 'I said no—'

Windleberry vaulted – hands-feet-hands-and-*fly* forward – feet first, like a missile at the Enemy's face. But the Enemy was no longer there. He hit the far wall, gathered himself and looked up – into the falling hammer!

WHAM!

He flung himself aside. Brass crashed into the crystal floor, and the floor crumbled. Windleberry fell through and his enemy fell with him. They grappled in midair.

'Hey, guys!' called Sally through the hole. 'I'm getting a *headache* here!'

Windleberry tumbled down the broad stairs. He had his hands on the hammer. It burned. With a mighty heave, he tore it from his enemy's grasp. He bent it into a pretzel-shape and threw it at the fiend's head.

The Enemy screamed in rage.

'GNAAARRRRRRGHAGH AGHHH!'

'Is anyone listening to me?' said Sally.

BLAM!

'TAKE THAT!'

KAWEEENG!

'OW!'

'Forget it,' said Sally. 'I'm going to bed.'

21: A PILLOW OF BROKEN GLASS

Slowly she climbed the stairs. She felt very out of place. She was wandering around the house in her pyjamas when she should be in bed. And as for the muffins – hadn't she been going to put them in the oven? But she had put them in the fridge instead.

It was just that her subtle, clever bid for freedom hadn't actually seemed so subtle or clever after all. Not when she had got there and looked at it. It had seemed the sort of thing a four-year-old would do.

Except four-year-olds were too sensible, she thought wearily. You had to wait to reach fourteen before you got this dumb.

What a choice:

Cat / Burn Muffins

Cat / Burn Muffins

Somehow she had ended up with 'cat'.

So what was she going to do now? Sleep? How was she going to sleep, feeling the way she did?

None of it made sense. Only the cat, warm and purring in her arms, seemed real. And if she let him spend the night in her room, he wouldn't just settle down quietly. He'd be poking his face into hers whenever he thought things were getting boring.

'You're a fat slob, Shades,' she murmured.

'Grrr,' replied Shades happily.

She got them both to her room. She found her way to the bed and turned back the duvet. She lay down and put her head on her pillow. Shades settled beside her, pushed her nose with his and sneezed over her face.

'Stop it,' groaned Sally. 'I'm trying to think.'

She had been going to do something. She hadn't exactly decided *not* to do it, but she hadn't done it.

Sometimes, not deciding something is a decision in itself.

Poot! went something very small in her ear. So small she did not notice it. And then something very small tumbled through the air and landed *Plop!* on her pillow. She didn't notice that either.

*

Muddlespot did.

He came sliding down the cat's hairy haunch at speed and scuttled over to where the thing had landed. It was . . .

'Corozin?' he gasped.

Stunned, battered and very much the worse for wear, the figure of Corozin lay full length upon the pillow and did not stir.

Muddlespot looked up, up the cliff face that was the side of Sally's head, to the ear from which Corozin had fallen. 'He did it! That Fluffy did it! Amazing!'

He looked at his prostrate master. He turned away. He took three paces and turned again.

Then he ran up *one-two-three* and kicked the fiend smartly on the butt. Corozin twitched, gratifyingly. Muddlespot danced away, snapping his fingers, to the fall of Sally's hair. Eagerly, he began to climb.

The mind of Sally Jones that night was like the scene of some disaster. Smoke hung in the corridors. Piles of crystal rubble were scattered everywhere. In the chambers, small crowds of ideas huddled together for comfort, clinging to each other and sobbing out their stories. The lights flickered on and off. Alarms were wailing in the distance and no one knew how to stop them.

'Windleberry did it,' breathed Muddlespot. He could hardly believe it was true.

He passed a row of statues. Two were headless and one had been broken off at the knees. A great hole gaped in the wall behind them. It looked very Corozin-shaped.

'Amazing!'

A clutch of hysterical ideas barged past him and ran down a stairway screaming. They seemed to be mathematical equations, but for some reason they were carrying hockey sticks. The fountain below the central chamber was choked with rubble. On the stairs, Muddlespot found the remains of Corozin's brass hammer. He picked it up and tried to unbend it. He couldn't.

Sally herself was not in the central chamber, but Windleberry was. He had a broom in his hands and was quietly sweeping up a pile of glass rubble.

'You did it!' cried Muddlespot.

Windleberry turned.

It was a Windleberry scarred by battle. His face was

bruised, his cream tuxedo was torn and his vermillion bow tie was badly rumpled. His magnificent Ray-Bans, when Muddlespot looked closely, had been reassembled with sticking plaster.

But it was Windleberry as was, undefeated. His shoulders were square. His head was more or less (give or take the odd swelling) square. His teeth – those he had left – were square. He towered over the little imp.

'Er, you're not going to do that to *me*, are you?' said Muddlespot.

'Too right I am,' said Windleberry. He thrust the broom under Muddlespot's nose. 'Unless you *instantly* take this out of my hands and get sweeping.'

Muddlespot's hands closed on it. 'Deal,' he said.

'This is nice, you know,' he added, as he began to brush up the fragments of the statue of Trufe. 'Just you and me. No bosses.'

Windleberry was examining the statue of Fairness. It had fallen from its pedestal. The base was damaged, but . . .

He bent down, picked up the statue by the shoulders and heaved.

'It's better to keep things *local*, don't you think?'

said Muddlespot. 'Nobody interfering, from your place or mine?'

'Shut up and sweep,' said Windleberry.

Clunk went the statue as it was set on its feet again. It wobbled a bit. Windleberry gave it a fierce look. It stopped wobbling, sheepishly.

'. . . I want this place cleared up by morning,' he said, turning away.

'You think you had it hard?' said Muddlespot. 'I had to sell my soul to a *cat*!'

The statue of Fairness tumbled once more from its pedestal.

Some things could be mended. Some couldn't. Some could be patched up. Other places had to be taped off with yellow warning tape and marked DON'T GO HERE! HEALING PROCESS AT WORK. Many ideas were homeless and had to be rehoused. Pretty much the whole of the French vocabulary corridor was uninhabitable, so entire families of verbs, declensions, subjunctives and irregulars got herded in together wherever there was space. Sally's French grades would not recover for a month.

It was during this part of the night that they noticed

that the trap door had gone from the little room just behind the central chamber. Windleberry frowned.

'Well, we can put the pin numbers and passwords in here,' said Muddlespot. 'Until we can get them properly sorted out, at least.'

'Hmm,' said Windleberry.

Muddlespot knew what was worrying him. Jumbling up the numbers would definitely cause problems later on, but it wasn't that. It was the trap door.

The trap door never went away. It might move, but it would always be somewhere. If there was one thing worse than having it close to the central chamber, it was not knowing where it was at all.

In the small hours, Muddlespot found it. He was rounding up some runaway Possible Boyfriends in the lower back rooms of Sally's mind, when, down a passage where the light flickered, he spotted a door.

He left the Boyfriends to their own devices – they were all pretty vague and shapeless, unlikely to do any harm – and tiptoed down to the door. Softly, he opened it and looked in.

There it was, in the middle of the floor. Closed. There was a lock on it. He looked at it and pursed his lips.

Locks could be opened, of course; that was the point of them.

But Sally would have the key.

He looked around the room. It was quite large, in fact. Dark. In the gloom he could make out a table, and against the walls there were cabinets and things. Little points of light showed here and there, as if from electric sockets. It might have been a kitchen.

There was a faint smell of burning in the air. It was not a smell that he could ever scrub away.

He closed the door softly and put some yellow tape across it. Not that he was changing sides or anything, but as he had said to Windleberry, he now firmly believed in keeping things *local*.

Then he picked up his broom and went whistling down the corridor in search of those Boyfriends. After all, one of them might come in useful one day.

22: MORNING

'Sally!' called Mum from downstairs. 'Are you awake?'

'No,' said Sally. At least, she thought she did.

'*Sally!*'

Sally sat up. It was light. The alarm said 7:15. When she had last looked at it, it had said 5:45. She must have slept, then. Finally. She groaned and got up. Shades was at the door, mewing pitifully to be let out. She opened it and watched him flit down the stairs in the direction of the kitchen.

Billie's door opened. Billie hurried out and down the stairs. 'Hi,' she said as she passed.

'What's the rush?' mumbled Sally.

'Baking the muffins for breakfast. Done you an extra one.'

'Oh . . . thanks,' said Sally.

The stairs were seeing a lot of traffic. Here came Mum, up from below. 'Morning, sweetheart. How do you feel?'

'Didn't sleep too well,' said Sally. 'But I'm OK now.'

'Glad to hear it. Have a hug. Mmmm. *Big* hug. Better?'

'Yeah, a bit. Can I have a bath?'

'Well . . .' Mum hesitated. 'A quick one. But you mustn't be late.'

'Cool.'

'You may be right, you know,' said Windleberry reluctantly. He was sitting side by side with Muddlespot, on the fallen statue of Fairness. The Inner Sally passed, towel in hand.

'No looking, you two,' she said.

Obediently they turned and sat facing the other way. Hot water splashed behind them. From somewhere the smell of fresh baking stole into the air.

'You pull your side,' said Windleberry, after a little while. 'I pull mine.'

'Yeah,' said Muddlespot. 'Nice. And easy.'

'She has to find her own way, in the end.'

'Yeah,' said Muddlespot. 'Keep it *warm*,' he added, dreamily.

'Muffins are done,' called someone from below. 'But the oven won't switch off again!'

'Oh God – Greg, you *have* to ring the electrician! No, do it now!'

Windleberry frowned. 'I wouldn't go *that* far. Mutual respect. Lines that can't be crossed. That kind of thing. But let's face it . . .'

'And *easy*,' murmured Muddlespot.

'What . . . ?'

Somewhere a voice called, 'Sally? Are you coming down?'

'They're calling you, Sally,' said Windleberry.

'Mmmmmm,' said Muddlespot.

'Sally?'

'Sally?'

There was no answer. The house was a jumble of voices. Billie hunting for her sports kit. Greg on the phone to the electrician. Mum calling. But it all seemed to be coming from very far away. Windleberry risked a look over his shoulder. 'You *fiend*!' he cried. 'You've sent her to sleep in the bath! We'll be late for school!'

Mum was knocking on the bathroom door. 'Sally? Are you coming down?'

'Sally! Wake up!' trumpeted Windleberry. 'SALLY? ARE YOU RECEIVING ME? ALERT! THIS IS AN EMERGENCY! ALERT!'

'You could try blowing soap up her nose,' said Muddlespot helpfully. 'That might work . . .'

So you dreamed of a city of fire and brass, and you've woken in lukewarm water with soap bubbles in your nose. And worse, you're late.

You tumble out of the bath, towel yourself off (a bit), chuck on your clothes (they stick to your wet skin) and . . .

. . . *start running!*

There *may* be a place like Pandemonium. There may not be.

There *may* be watchtowers above the clouds, where thousand-eyed angels look down on Earth and all that happens there. You'll think about that later.

But when you do think about it, maybe you'll find those places in other things. Little things. And not where you thought they were. In soap and warm water, maybe, and a quick doze after a bad night's sleep. These can seem pretty close to Heaven all by themselves. So can a hug on the landing, which says (without saying it), Let's Forget About Yesterday. And so can a freshly baked muffin. Even if you have to eat it while running down the pavement.

OK, so it's not really Heaven. But who wants to get to Heaven?

Like someone said: It's as good to travel as to arrive.